THE AMISH LIBRARY

AN AMISH ROMANCE

Naomi Troyer

Contents

Chapter 1 A Horse in a Ditch..3

Chapter 2 They All Fall Down..8

Chapter 3 A Flicker of Hope..13

Chapter 4 Wuthering Words 18

Chapter 5 Callouses & Commands 23

Chapter 6 Stronger Than a Hurricane..27

Chapter 7 Chasing Dreams 33

Chapter 8 Expectations & Demands..39

Chapter 9 Shooting Stars 45

Chapter 10 A Gift Horse..49

Chapter 11 Ironclad & Generous 54

Chapter 12 When the Cub Threatens the Lion 59

Chapter 13 A Cold Goodbye 66

Chapter 14 Intercepted Mail 70

Chapter 15 A Gift That Can Be Tamed 74

Chapter 16 A Stranger in Danger..78

Chapter 17 Shine Your Light 82

Chapter 18 The Serpent & The Light 86

Chapter 19 Blood is Thicker Than Water 90

Chapter 20 An Old Wives Tale 95

Chapter 21 A Courtship or a Breakup 99

Epilogue 103

Chapter 1
A Horse in a Ditch

In the small-town of Old Apple, just north of Zook's Corner, almost everyone knew about Josef's traveling library.

There was no mistaking Josef's buggy for any other, as every surface on his buggy contained bookshelves. He safely secured all the books with braided cords that were hooked onto the shelves, making sure it harmed the books as little as possible. They covered vast distances on most days of the week.

Josef's library had become a highlight for many Amish folks. He brought the written word right to their doorstep, for the cost of a single trade. You give one; you take one.

He never asked for money for his services and never complained about spending his days on the road.

In Annie Hauptfleisch's eyes, her father was the closest thing to a saint that had ever lived. He had always been kind and generous and that was why she still felt tears sting her eyes whenever the realization struck her again that her father was no longer around.

The heart attack had caught him in his sleep. He had barely woken up to clutch his chest before he was called to the heavenly gates. His absence left a large void in their family, as well as the rest of the community.

But Annie had vowed beside her father's grave that she would continue with his life's work to honor his memory. She would continue traveling with the library to make sure none of her father's readers were disappointed.

It had only been two weeks since her father had drawn his last breath, but Annie knew he wouldn't want her sitting at home wallowing in her grief. He would want her to make sure his readers received a new book without too much delay.

The trip her father drove every day was a round trip of about 40 miles. The traveling library served not only their community of Old Apple, it also served the Amish community south of town. Annie had accompanied her father many times on his route and knew it by heart, but that didn't mean her mother approved of her determination to continue with her father's legacy.

This morning when she had hitched the library buggy to the horse, her mother had only given her a single look, making it clear she didn't approve of Annie driving around on her own, especially not through the town of Old Apple.

Annie wasn't afraid of the long trip she needed to make, or of the traffic she needed to be careful of in Old Apple. She just regretted that her father wouldn't be sitting there beside her.

She had just finished making her rounds in their community and was now headed to the community south of town. She easily navigated through the town's traffic, knowing that Shakespeare, her father's trusted horse, knew the route just as well as she did.

As she held the reins, she found herself once again admiring her father's vision over twenty years ago.

Josef Hauptfleisch had inherited wealth when his parents had passed away. Seven farms and a healthy investment secured his financial future for life. Her father hadn't kept all the farms, instead he only kept the largest farm, one that he could farm without too much trouble. He had donated two of the farms to the community for joint farming ventures and had sold the other four farms before investing the money.

After realizing he was a very wealthy man, Josef did something to give back to the community. He had bought a truck load of books, all inspiration and motivational fiction, as well as some cookbooks and self-help books, before he had started the traveling library.

It had never earned him a single penny and yet he had loved every day he spent on the road bringing the written word to the Amish communities.

Selfless—is the word Annie always associated with her father.

When she and her brother, Amos, were younger, her father had farmed as well. But as Amos grew older, he took over the farming side of things while her father spent more days on the road with the library.

Now, it would be Annie spending her days on the road.

Not that she minded at all. She had always enjoyed riding around their beautiful town and the nearby community. She also loved knowing that she was bringing books to people who wouldn't read otherwise.

It was a humble avocation; one that Annie intended to continue with for the rest of her life.

She guided the horse left as they rode out of Old Apple. At the fork in the road, she veered right before she turned onto the dirt road.

In the distance, white houses dotted the landscape, accompanied by the odd red barn. It was from reading that knew why the barns were red. They hadn't been painted red, instead it was the type of oil farmers had been using for years to treat the wood that gave it the red appearance. Just like she had learned that from books, there were many other interesting facts and stories she had picked up through the years.

The weather was warm, with simply a breeze to keep most of the heat away. As the air moved past her, she could smell the sweet scent of the sugar maple trees in the distance. Captivated by the fragrance, Annie wondered if other people also related memories to scent.

The scent of freshly baked bread always reminded her of winter. Just like the scent of coffee reminded her of her father. You would barely ever catch him without a cup in his hand.

Powder and lavender were the scents that made her think of her mother...

Before Annie knew what was happening, the buggy swayed before it bumped its way right into a ditch on the side of the road. She heard books tumbling from their shelves, even as Shakespeare let out a loud whinny as if to make it clear it wasn't his fault.

Annie let out a heavy sigh as she shook her head. She had been distracted with her thoughts for a few seconds and look at what had happened.

She had steered Shakespeare directly into a ditch!

Chapter 2
They All Fall Down

Levi Hertzler glanced over at his brother and let out a sigh. By just looking at Abram Hertzler, you could see he loved the land and drew pleasure from working it. Levi had never found that connection with the land or that excitement in a good harvest.

Not that he minded the hard work, he simply didn't have a passion for farming like his younger brother did. They differed with only three years, but the difference was vast when you compared their personalities.

Levi would much rather read about the world and try to improve their methods, whereas it would bore Abram after just a few pages.

Levi enjoyed his company and had no problem being alone for most of the time, but Abram preferred the company of others.

And so the list continued.

A very, very long list.

The brothers often joked about how they can't truly be related, but regardless of their differences, they shared a bond stronger than most. Abram respected Levi's knowledge gained from books and Levi appreciated his brother's insight with the farm.

In the distance, Levi noticed the Josef's traveling library. A smile curved the corners of his mouth. Tonight he could embark on a new journey. Usually, Josef stopped by their farm at least once a week, but it had been two weeks since his last stop.

Levi had eagerly been awaiting the old man's visit, especially since he had read all the books in his possession twice already. He turned to his brother. "Abram, I'll be back shortly. Just going to exchange my books."

"You and your books. Just hurry before Daed gets back," Abram called back.

It was a well-known fact in their family that Isaac Hertzler didn't appreciate his eldest son's love for books. He would constantly remind Levi that there was a time when the ordnung prohibited reading of any nature unless it was the bible.

That the ordnung had amended the rules regarding reading over fifteen years ago was a mistake in his father's eyes. Regardless of his father's objections, Levi loved to read. He wasn't naïve and knew very well the risks that could come with literature, especially contemporary literature and fiction.

But his father hadn't ever even asked him what he read.

Levi's preferences were towards the Amish fiction that Josef carried, as well as books on nature, health, natural remedies, and livestock. Josef didn't carry any material the bishop would frown upon.

Not like the library in town.

Levi rushed into his bedroom and collected the three books on his nightstand. He grabbed an apple from the kitchen table before he headed towards the gate to meet Josef Hauptfleisch. By the time Levi reached the gate at the entrance of their property, it surprised him to see that Josef's buggy was no longer moving.

A frown creased his brow as he moved closer for a better view. But with every step he took, the problem became clearer.

Josef had steered the horse into a ditch just beside their fence line. Many of the braided cords that secured the books had come loose, causing books to be scattered in the ditch, the road, and some even lying in the field beyond the fence.

It hurt Levi's heart to see all the books lying around, and he knew Josef would be just as concerned. He headed to towards the buggy with a quickened pace, eager to help. He already knew that Josef would inspect every book's cover and binding to make sure they hadn't been damaged.

"Hullo Shakespeare," Levi greeted Josef's horse and was rewarded with a grunt of recognition. "Jah, I brought your apple," Levi laughed as he held out the apple and Shakespeare gobbled it up. He glanced at the buggy and saw the wheel in the ditch. Without the weight of the books, it would be easy enough to lift the buggy out, he estimated as he rubbed Shakespeare's flank.

Levi had a good idea of how far Shakespeare had to travel every day and always treated him to an apple or fresh drink of water. "Josef?" Levi called out, moving around the buggy.

As he walked, he collected books. There was a scuffed cover here, a torn page there, but otherwise the books seemed to have survived the fall. "Josef?" Levi called out again, wondering if the elderly man have fallen from the buggy and suffered an injury.

Just as he reached the back of the buggy, he heard a female voice.

"He… he isn't here. It's just me."

She looked up at him with tears streaming down her face, her blonde braid hanging over her shoulder, having escaped from her prayer kapp.

For a moment Levi could do nothing but stare. She looked beautiful and so very sad that it made his heart ache. "I uh… I'm Levi Hertzler," Levi finally said, not knowing how to respond.

Levi knew the books were valuable, but he couldn't imagine why she would cry over them as if they were about to be buried.

She nodded with a sad smile. "I'm Annie Hauptfleisch, Josef's dochder."

"It's a pleasure to meet you, Annie," Levi said, handing her the books he had collected. "Is your daed not here today?"

Annie shook her head and set the books down on a pile she had been making. "Nee… he… he passed."

Levi winced before empathy rushed over him. "I'm terribly sorry for your loss. When the library didn't come, I just thought… it doesn't matter. My prayers will be with your familye, your daed was a very gut mann."

"Denke," Annie said, sniffing back her tears. "And I just made a mess of his library on my very first day on the road. "He passed away in his sleep, a heart attack, the doctors said."

Levi could see how the grief weighted down her shoulders as she spoke. "I'm so sorry."

She quietly cried and for the first time, Levi wanted to console a total stranger. He'd never met Josef's daughter before, but he felt as if he knew her from everything her father had told him.

He knew she loved books, he knew she was kind and right now he knew she was struggling to come to terms with the death of her father.

"Here, let me help you," Levi offered, knowing that his father would return from town at any moment. But right now he didn't care about his father's wrath. He cared about the beautiful sad girl that stood before him lost in a maze of heartache.

Chapter 3
A Flicker of Hope

This morning when she had left home, Annie had sworn that she wouldn't cry today. She allowed her grief to keep her from riding her father's library buggy for two weeks, and today would've been the day she managed without breaking down in tears.

But the moment she saw the books, all that her father had touched and loved, scattered in the road, the ditch and just beyond the fence, it felt as if she had let her father down.

As if she had lost him all over again.

It suddenly reminded her that every book she had given out today would be a book her father would never again touch. That realization, along with her momentary distraction landing her in a ditch, seemed to have opened the faucets on her heartache, and she couldn't seem to stop the tears from coming.

Through the tears she glanced at Levi Hauptfleisch and felt humiliated that he had found her like this. She knew exactly what she needed to do, but couldn't seem to stop crying long enough to do it. Instead, it was as if her heart was breaking all over again, even as the doubts grew in her mind. Had her mother been right? Was a traveling library a too big a task for a woman? Was it really a mann's work?

"You don't have to..." Annie argued as Levi collected the books. "I can manage."

Levi smiled up at her in a way that made her heart skip a beat. For a moment she forgot about the books laying in the dirt, too overwhelmed by the shock of attraction she felt bolting through her body.

He was tall, taller than most of the boys she had seen at Sunday singings, and although his hair was dark, his eyes a shade of coffee brown, and his features strong and cold, there was something about him that made Annie feel as if she could confide in him, or at least trust him.

"I want to. I was very fond of your daed and grateful for the traveling library. It's my pleasure," Levi said as he broke eye contact.

Together, they gathered all the books and piled them beside the buggy. Once all the books were collected, Annie stood to guide Shakespeare, while Levi guided the wheel out of the ditch.

The horse tugged and struggled a little at first until finally he pulled the buggy free.

"Denke!" Annie cried out gratefully. "Now I just have to load these and secure them, then I'll be on my way."

"Here, let me help," Levi offered.

They worked side by side until all the books were back on their shelves. Levi ensured to secure the hooks on the braided elastic bands. "There you go, all set for your next stop."

"Denke. Did you want to exchange books?" Annie asked, feeling flustered after the chaos of the last fifteen minutes.

"Jah, denke I almost forgot." Levi browsed through the shelves, and Annie couldn't help but follow him with her gaze.

The books he returned were quite interesting. She had read all of them before. She couldn't help but wonder which books he would choose today.

"I completely lost track of the books I wanted to get today," Levi said, turning to her with a foolish smile.

Annie returned his smile. "What do you usually enjoy?"

"A fiction book, a little poetry, something about nature. Actually, I'm so starved for reading, I might just read anything you give me," Levi admitted with a shrug.

"Then I have just what you need," Annie said, feeling empowered. A few moments ago she had felt so helpless. She had thought her mother had been right. Perhaps she wasn't responsible enough to handle the traveling library, but now…. Just maybe she was.

She collected a few books and returned to Levi where he stood rubbing Shakespeare. "Here. What do you think of these?"

She handed him the books and felt she was on the mark when he smiled at the Shakespeare play right at the top. "It's one of his lesser-known plays, but I found it very humorous. You'll also see a collection of poems from the eighteenth century. Although some of them are hard to understand, I found them to be gems."

"This is… exactly what I was looking for. And this?" Levi asked, turning over a book about gardening to read the back.

"It's not your usual gardening book. It's a book about diseases on vegetables. How to spot them before they ruin your crop, how to use kitchen remedies to stop the diseases…" Annie stopped when he looked at her as if she were a genius.

"You truly have your daed's instinct for choosing books," Levi complimented her with a smile.

Annie felt her shoulders swell just a little at the compliment. She knew she could never fill her father's shoes with the traveling library, but perhaps she might just be able to fill some of it. Suddenly she was no longer angry at herself for landing the buggy in a ditch, instead she was grateful she had taken the traveling library on its route today.

"Denke. You might also enjoy the book at the bottom of the pile. It's an Amish mystery that plays out in Ohio. A little sleuthing and mystery, but not too much. I know my daed always enjoyed a little mystery," Annie explained.

"Then I'll take these four, unless I can only take three?" Levi asked hopefully.

Annie smiled. The general rule was only three books at a time, but Levi had just helped her save the buggy and the books. "Four books are fine. I'll come around next week again. Denke for your help."

"Denke, for continuing with the traveling library. I wouldn't read if it wasn't for the library buggy."

Annie nodded, understanding. "That's why Daed began it. Goodbye."

"Goodbye to you, Annie, and no more driving into ditches. I think you scared Shakespeare enough for one day."

Annie's laughter carried on the sugar maple scented breeze as she took the reins. Her day might have started filled with doubts, but now she couldn't help but feel hopeful about her endeavor. Regardless of her mother's objections, the traveling library had become part of the lives of many people.

Annie knew her father wouldn't want it to stop.

She planned on continuing her father's legacy, even if she had to beg her mother every time she took the reins.

Chapter 4
Wuthering Words

The only person Levi could ever share his love for reading with had been Josef. Josef had encouraged him to open his mind to new books and to find what he enjoyed most.

But after meeting Annie, Levi couldn't help but feel that she had a gift. The books she had suggested for him to read had kept him captivated and intrigued. He had laughed and done some soul-searching and, more than anything, he had enjoyed them.

All four books were books he never would've chosen on his own. If it hadn't been for her suggestions, he would've looked them over. Levi had appreciated Josef, but he appreciated Annie even more. She understood his mind and his hunger for the written word better than he did.

He thought about that and wrote her a note.

The note turned into a whole page. As soon as Levi explained what he most enjoyed about the books she had suggested for him to read, he couldn't stop. He quoted excerpts from the poems, explaining to her how they had meant more to him than he had imagined.

Levi wanted her to know that he appreciated her suggestions and that she was doing the right thing by continuing the traveling library buggy in honor of her father's legacy.

All four books were finished by Monday and was eagerly waiting to see the traveling library coming towards their farm. Monday passed with no sight of Annie or her library. Tuesday, he kept his eye on the road the entire day.

Levi had left his books by the front door, so that he could just rush in and grab them before meeting Annie when she arrived. But by Tuesday late afternoon, Levi realized he would probably have to wait another day to trade his books.

It was shortly before lunch on Wednesday when he looked up from weeding the cornfields, only to see her buggy traveling down the dirt road.

Levi's heart skipped a beat, something it had never done before at the thought of getting a new book. As he made his way to the house, he wondered if his excitement was just about the books, or perhaps Annie as well.

He shrugged the idea away, knowing he couldn't possibly be excited to see a girl he barely knew, before he grabbed the books and ran towards the road.

Annie pulled the buggy over just as he arrived. She climbed down with a friendly smile. "Hullo Levi."

"Hullo Annie," Levi said, bursting to tell her how much he had enjoyed the books.

She accepted the books from him and gestured to the buggy. "What do you feel like reading this week?"

Levi shrugged with a smile. "The books you gave me were amazing. Perhaps you have a few more suggestions?"

Levi could see something troubled Annie today. He didn't know her well enough to pry, but couldn't help but be concerned. "Is everything all right?"

Annie nodded with a sad smile. "Jah, everything is fine. My mamm was just upset this morning when I told her I was taking the library out again. She insists it's too dangerous for me to do on my own."

"Dangerous?" Levi asked curiously before he remembered Josef had stayed in the community on the other side of town. "I guess the traffic in town could be a little hindersome."

"Jah, it could. Especially if you have a young horse who isn't used to cars and horns blaring. But Shakespeare has been doing this route forever. Unless I guide him into a ditch, he'll travel the entire route without getting lost," Annie explained.

Levi nodded. "Your daed always praised Shakespeare's gut disposition."

"Jah, he raised him from a foal, you know..." Annie moved towards the horse and rubbed his neck. "Shakespeare and I are just about the same age."

Levi couldn't help but be curious how old that would be. He searched Annie's features and looked for a sign that she might have a sweetheart or a husband. He wasn't one to pry, but he couldn't help but wonder that if she was married if her husband had an opinion about the library buggy.

"Does your mann also fear when you take out the library?" he heard himself asking.

Annie laughed and shook her head. "Unless I forgot I have one, I'm single."

"Gut." As soon as the words left Levi's mouth, he realized how foolish it would be of him to like Annie. She lived in another community and he barely knew her.

Annie blushed and turned towards the library buggy. "Let's see what I can suggest for you today."

Levi hadn't yet courted and at twenty-three, it was quite unusual for an Amish man. But until now, he'd met no one he wanted to ask on a buggy ride. Annie's cheeks turned a light pink and he couldn't help but think her prettier because of it. "Something just as gut as last time."

Annie laughed. "I see I've set high expectations."

"That you have," Levi agreed.

Annie searched through the books and finally selected one. "Here, I think this will agree with you. I especially liked the characters. They're not overwritten and not superficial. They're real people with genuine problems and the ending… it's completely unexpected. I'll keep quiet now before I spoil it for you."

For the next ten minutes, Annie repeated the process. Finally, Levi had three books that he knew he would enjoy.

He also knew that he would think of Annie when he read them.

"Denke. I look forward to reading them," Levi said, not wanting her to leave just yet. He glanced back at the field where Abram was working and knew he couldn't stay much longer.

"Just don't blame me if you don't get any sleep. That first one is really a page-turner. The history about the Amish… and how they came to settle here… It's truly fascinating."

Levi smiled. "I'm sure it is. I... there's a note in the book's front I returned. Just my thoughts on the books I read."

Annie's face lit up with surprise. "Really, I look forward to reading it. Have a gut week, Levi."

"You too, Annie," Levi said before he turned to the horse. "You take gut care of her Shakespeare, no more ditches."

Annie's laughter filled his heart with happiness as she took the reins. "Shakespeare and I have a new agreement. I pretend to hold the reins and he pretends to obey my commands. That way, we both get home safely."

Levi chuckled at her humor. "Sounds like a gut plan."

"Good bye," Annie called over her shoulder as Shakespeare walked.

For a few moments, Levi watched her drive away. He found himself intrigued and charmed by Annie, more than he had been by any other girl before.

He glanced down at the books in his hands and knew that he couldn't wait to read. Because in the past when he read, he felt his horizons broaden, now when he read, he felt himself learning more about Annie.

With a whistle and a skip in his step, Levi returned to his work in the fields.

Chapter 5
Callouses & Commands

"Annie, look at your hands!" Rebecca Hauptfleisch cried out in horror.

Annie had no choice but to follow her hands as her mother grabbed them and headed straight for the kitchen sink. "Mamm, it's not that bad."

"Callouses are one thing–they're a sign of hard work. But dirty callouses, ach nee Annie. How must a mann ever find your hands attractive when they look like this?" Rebecca clucked her tongue as she scrubbed Annie's hands.

Annie knew that arguing would only make her mother more adamant to prove her point, so instead she stood by helplessly as her mother washed her hands until they stung from all the scrubbing.

"There, now you put some lotion on that, you hear?" Rebecca finally let go of Annie's hands.

Annie did as she was told and returned to the kitchen, ready to help her mother with dinner.

"Anything I can do, Mamm?" Annie asked.

Her mother set down the paring knife and took a seat at the kitchen table. "Jah, you can sit down with me."

Annie felt an overwhelming feeling of dread come over her. "Jah, Mamm?"

Rebecca let out a heavy sigh as she searched her daughter's gaze. "Annie, I know how close you and your daed were. I know you shared your love for books. I also know that you're only continuing with the traveling library to keep his memories alive."

Annie felt her throat close up with tears. She'd once heard that grieving tears were when you had too much love in your heart for someone you had lost. Without being able to give that love to the person, it simply welled up until it spilled over in your eyes. Right now, that described exactly how Annie felt.

"But Annie," Rebecca said a little kindlier as she reached for her daughter's hand. "Your daed wouldn't have wanted this. He wouldn't have wanted you to spend your days traveling thirty miles or more just to lend books. His whole life, all he wanted for you, was a gut husband. A mann that will care and provide for you just like he did. How will you find that when you spend all your time on that buggy and you refuse to attend singings?"

Annie sighed. "Mamm… I've told you before, I don't believe in searching for love. When the time is right, the right mann will cross my path. Until then, I will not sit around and moisturize my hands just waiting for him to arrive."

"Ach! You're as stubborn as your daed. What you don't realize is the traveling library was an idea we both had together. But I knew right from the start that it's too dangerous for a woman to spend her days alone on a buggy. That's why your daed did it," Rebecca explained.

Annie's gaze softened. "But you also had me and Amos to care for. I don't have kinner, Mamm. I want to do this. Daed always said that the traveling library was his way of giving back. They blessed him with a wealthy inheritance and knew that not everyone had that gut fortune. I'm also blessed by being born into this familye. I've never had to work a day in my life. Amos works the fields and the farm because it's his passion. Books are my passion."

"I know they are Annie, and I know we are all blessed. But surely your daed wouldn't have wanted this…. Do you really think he would've expected you to spend all of your time in a buggy with only Shakespeare for company?" Rebecca asked with a cocked brow.

Annie shrugged. "Shakespeare makes for gut company. He never complains when I recite Shakespeare," Annie teased.

Her mother smiled, but it didn't reach her eyes. "I just don't think it's a gut idea for you to continue the traveling library. I just lost your daed Annie. I can't stand the thought of losing you as well."

Annie could understand her mother's fear, but she wanted to continue to honor her father's legacy. "Mamm, Gott already knows when it will be time for me to enter the heavenly gates. Besides, I'm not afraid of traveling through Old Apple. Everyone knows the book buggy. They even wave at me as I drive through. I won't stop, Mamm, but I will promise you to be very careful." Annie glanced down at her red-scrubbed hands. "And I will wear gloves when I hold the reins."

Rebecca laughed. "You're just like your daed. Always too clever to argue with. Just remember Annie…" her mother's eyes narrowed. "Until the day you are wed, you are my responsibility. You don't always have to like what my opinion is, but you will respect it."

Annie swallowed, knowing her mother was clarifying that she was being understood. But if the day came that her mother insisted she stop the book exchange, she wouldn't have any other choice. "Jah Mamm."

"Gut. Now you wash up and check on your books while I start on dinner."

Annie did as she was told. She headed to the buggy and made sure she organized all the books in order of genre, before she remembered the note Levi had left for her.

She pulled it out of the book and smiled as she read. Was it strange that the reasons she suggested the titles to him was the same reasons he enjoyed it?

Annie had never felt herself understand anyone more, or more connected to anyone that wasn't family. It might be a few days before she would head to the Hertzler farm again, but until then, Annie at least had Levi's words to keep her company.

That, and Shakespeare, of course.

Chapter 6
Stronger Than
a Hurricane

Despite her mother's protestations, Annie continued with the traveling library. For the first time she met so many people, it felt as if she was living in one of the books she always liked to escape to.

She had met a widow who didn't have any family, who always waited for Annie with tea and cookies. Annie stayed happily to keep the widow company, and Shakespeare also didn't complain about the brief rest.

Then there was the bishop's daughter, who read only books about their Amish history and faith. She planned on one day following in her father's footsteps, or at least to become a deacon in their community.

After a few weeks of traveling the roads her father had travelled for so many years, Annie realized that it wasn't only about the books. These people had become her father's friends—for some of them, her father was the only person they would see come to their door.

Apart from for bringing them books, her father had also brought them company, a shoulder to lean on, and most of all he had been a friend to some of the loneliest people Annie had ever met.

When she had taken over the traveling library, she had been convinced she could do the entire route in two days, but now Annie knew it wasn't about how fast she could cover the route, but to plan her route according to those that wanted to visit and those that didn't.

Unconsciously, she planned her trip to the community south of town to include a brief visit with Levi. The houses were far apart in his community, some almost up on the hills where the tree line met the farms, but Levi always welcomed them with a smile and an apple for Shakespeare.

Today the weather was warm enough that Annie could smell Shakespeare's sweat from the buggy. "I'll give you a nice wash this afternoon when we get home, Shakespeare." Annie promised from her seat on the buggy.

She already knew that on days like today, Levi would offer that Shakespeare have a drink of water and rest in the shade for a little before she continued.

Just like she had hoped, Levi was waiting for her by the water trough when she arrived.

"I thought Shakespeare might like a drink," Levi called out with greeting.

Annie smiled with a nod. "He would. We've taken it slow today because of the heat, but even I feel like a desert."

"I thought you would," Levi said, gesturing to the table on the porch. "I have some fresh sun tea that is ice cold."

Annie almost cried with joy. "That sounds wunderbaar."

Ever since the first time Levi had left a note to share his thoughts on the books she had recommended, he continued to do it every time Annie stopped by. She no longer waited to see him before she made recommendations, instead she handpicked books she thought he would enjoy as other readers returned them.

Once Shakespeare was happily standing in the shade, gulping away, she collected the parcel of books on the buggy seat and followed Levi up to the porch.

An older man approached the porch with a curious look. "Hullo, I don't think we've met. I'm Levi's daed, Isaac."

"It's a pleasure to meet you, Isaac. I'm Annie Hauptfleisch," Annie held out her hand with a smile.

"Annie is Josef's dochder. She's taken over the traveling library ever since her daed passed on," Levi explained as he handed Annie a glass of ice-cold sun tea.

"That's a lot of responsibility for a young girl. You couldn't be a day older than fourteen?" Isaac said with a curious look.

Annie laughed. She was used to people mistaking her age. "Actually, I'm turning twenty-one in the fall. But denke for the compliment."

"Ah, I see. And no sweetheart that is complaining about you visiting with my seeh?" Isaac fired the next question.

Annie couldn't help but feel as if Levi's father didn't approve of her being there. She kept her smile in place and nodded towards the horse. "Levi was kind enough to offer Shakespeare a drink of water. We came all the way from the community north of town. I thought I'd give him a rest before we continue to the widow Baker."

"The widow Baker?" Isaac asked, surprised. "You do travel far."

Annie nodded. "Jah, but Shakespeare is a wunderbaar horse. He never complains. I think he enjoys the route just as much as I do."

"Well… you travel safe, young lady. And you're welcome to stop here before you head back if he needs another drink of water," Isaac offered with a change of attitude.

Annie smiled. "Denke. It was nice meeting you, Isaac."

As soon as Levi's father disappeared into the kitchen, Levi turned to her with a doubtful look. "My daed isn't very fond of my reading. He thinks it's a waste of time."

Annie sighed. It was like that with many of the older members in the Amish communities. Some of them could barely read themselves, and others were young at a time when reading was prohibited unless it was material from the school house. "I always wish I could find the right book for someone like that. A book that will teach them the value of words and open their minds to the joy it can bring."

Levi chuckled. "I doubt such a book exists for my daed."

"Your mamm, does she read?" Annie asked, finishing the last of her sun tea.

Levi shook his head. "She used to, she taught me to read and I guess I inherited my love of reading from her. But she passed… over ten years ago."

"I'm sorry to hear that," Annie sympathized.

"It was mercy—she had been suffering from cancer," Levi explained.

Annie could see from the pained look in his eyes that this wasn't something that Levi discussed every day. She couldn't help but feel privileged he had shared it with her. "Here are your books," she handed him the bundle of books she had tied with a ribbon.

"Same recipe as always," Levi chuckled as he read the spines. "Mystery, faith, self-help, and poetry."

Annie nodded with a smile as she stood up. "I don't believe there is much in the world that mystery, faith, and poetry couldn't save. And the self-help books empower us to do just that, effect change."

Levi stood up and for a moment, they were barely a foot apart. As she noticed the dark brown coffee color of his eyes, Annie caught her breath. "Annie, you changed me..."

Annie felt her heart skip a beat. It was such a profound thing to say and if she hadn't been shy, she would have told Levi that he'd changed her as well. She loved hearing his thoughts on her favorite reads, but more than that, she felt changed by the connection she felt with him. "I better start going. The widow Baker is probably waiting for us."

Levi cleared his throat and stepped back with a smile. "You drive safe, Annie, and thank you for these."

"It's a pleasure. I hope you enjoy them."

As Annie climbed back into the buggy and took the reins, she wondered what had just happened. She had read about attraction and love in the poetry collections that her father had purchased for the traveling library, but she had never experienced it before.

She had read about it being a force stronger than a hurricane, faster than a tornado, and fiercer than a mother's instinct...

Now she realized all those comparisons hadn't just been pretty summations of an emotion she didn't understand.

They were all understatements of an emotion she had just experienced for the first time.

Her heart was dancing in her chest as she directed Shakespeare out of the Hertzler yard. Suddenly, Annie couldn't wait to see Levi again. She wanted to know if what she had just experienced had been a onetime encounter, or if next time she would feel it again.

She might not be ready to court or want to search for love like her mother had advised her to, but Annie was more than ready to explore an emotion stronger than any emotion she had ever felt before.

Chapter 7
Chasing Dreams

Levi looked forward to Annie's every visit. She had become the friend he had never had. Of course, he had many friends in his community, but none that understood his love for reading.

For the first time he had someone that shared that passion, that understood that hunger, and Levi found that more attractive than any physical feature he'd ever admired on a woman.

He admired Annie's mind.

Although she was from a different community, they shared the same values and Levi fell a little more for her every time he saw her.

Today was one of those hot days, where the morning started with sweat beading on your chest even before you rolled out of bed. By mid-morning, the sun was burning down on his back in the fields where he worked with his brother.

His father was in the barn, mucking out the stalls and doing chores around the house to avoid the scorching heat of the fields.

Here and there the cornfields offered blissful shade against the heat, but Levi knew Annie wouldn't have that privilege. Neither would Shakespeare. By the time they broke for lunch, Levi was hot and wished he could sneak away with Abram for a quick dip in the spring, but instead he stayed home.

His father went to lie down and rest for an hour, but Levi didn't do that either.

Instead, he filled the trough with fresh water for Shakespeare, set out some hay and prepared a fresh jug of sun tea with lots of ice. He knew Annie would be just as grateful as Shakespeare for the rest and to quench her thirst.

He waited for her beneath the large oak tree where the water trough stood. The week before, he had used the draught horse and ropes to drag two large logs to the tree. Now he and Annie could sit in the cool shade and talk about books while Shakespeare slaked his thirst.

Levi knew her routine and knew that on Wednesdays she usually stopped by after lunch. He hoped he had his timing right, because as soon as Abram returned from the creek and his father stood up from his rest, it would be back to the fields.

He had barely taken a seat when he saw Shakespeare and the library buggy coming down the road. An excitement unlike Levi had ever known washed over him as he waited for them beneath the tree.

Annie's smile was broad and made his heart skip a beat. Her light blonde hair was neatly braided beneath her prayer kapp, Levi noticed when she climbed down from the buggy. "Hullo Levi. Shakespeare has been looking forward to this stop for an hour."

Levi smiled as he brushed the horse's flank. "He deserves it for taking such gut care of you."

Annie sighed as she moved to sit down on the log. "It might not be for long, though."

"Is he sick?" Levi asked concerned before glancing towards the horse.

Annie shook her head. "Nee, there's nothing wrong with Shakespeare. He still has the energy of a filly and the strength of a five-year-old. It's my mamm…."

Levi poured them each a glass of iced-tea. "Is she ill?"

Annie smiled sadly. "Nee, she isn't ill either. But she insists that the thought of me on the road most days is making her ill…" Annie took a long drink of her tea before she met Levi's gaze again. "She wants me to stop the book exchange."

Levi's eyes widened with horror. For the first time, he realized that although he looked forward to reading new books, he looked forward to seeing Annie even more. "But why?"

"Because it's dangerous. She would prefer to have me home where she can watch over me. I don't know all the reasons; I just know that every time I hitch the library buggy to Shakespeare, she gets angry." Annie let out a heavy sigh. "I don't know what I'm going to do. This was my daed's life's work and now it might all go to waste…"

"Annie, please don't be sad," Levi said encouragingly. It hurt him to see her so sad. "I'm sure she's just trying to deal with her grief. Perhaps in time she'll understand…"

"I don't think so. She threatened to sell the buggy if I didn't see reason. How long before she makes gut on that threat?" Annie's eyes shone with tears. "What am I going to do?"

Levi thought for a moment before a smile curved the corners of his mouth. "We're going to pray for a miracle. Annie, we've read about so many miracles. We've read stories where characters faced the impossible only for a miracle to save them. That's what you need." Levi didn't add that he needed it as well.

Without seeing Annie, he already knew his world would slowly fall apart. He had feelings for her and nothing made him realize that more than the chance that he wouldn't see her again.

"I know we serve a Gott that can make miracles happen, but I feel foolish praying for one, Levi. There are sick people, people facing poverty and so much worse that need a miracle more than I do." Annie's humility made Levi like her even more.

"Annie, Gott doesn't hold back on miracles for special occasions or dire situations. He blesses everyone with them. We just have to believe. Cast your worries on to me… Remember, that is what he says in his scripture. Perhaps that's exactly what you need to do. Besides, I can't see Shakespeare being happy standing in a field all day. I think he enjoys these daily trips just as much as you do."

Annie laughed as she glanced at the horse. "He does, definitely. The widow Baker has taken to treating him with sugar cubes. As soon as I pull into her yard, he whinnies, as if to pronounce his arrival."

Levi chuckled. "He's a special horse, just like your daed was a special man. It takes a special woman to take that place. And you're that woman, Annie."

Their gazes locked and for a moment Levi was certain he saw the same affection in Annie's gaze as he felt in his heart. It was too soon for him to even consider acting on his feelings, but the look in her gaze gave him hope.

"Ever since I could remember, I wanted to take over the traveling library. My bruder has always enjoyed working in the field more than reading. I knew he wouldn't be interested, but now it feels as if my dreams are crumbling before my eyes. Can you imagine if someone told you you could no longer farm?" Annie asked, curiously.

Levi considered his answer for a moment. He hadn't ever lied to Annie by omission before and couldn't imagine himself starting now. If he wanted this friendship to last, he needed to trust Annie with his dreams as well. "Actually… Farming has never been a dream for me, like taking over the library buggy is for you."

"It isn't? But your crops look wunderbaar. You definitely put a lot of work into it," Annie said, a little confused.

"My bruder, Abram, is the true farmer. Actually…" Levi drew in a deep breath, summoning his courage before he spoke his heart's deepest wish out loud. "I've always dreamed of becoming a writer. Not a self-help writer or someone documenting the past. Instead, I've always wanted to become an inspirational Christian writer. I want to write stories that inspire people to live closer to Gott. Stories that strengthen their fate and make them believe that regardless of the challenges they face, there is a way for Gott to help.

I've already got a few ideas of what I want my first book to be about… but I guess I've accepted it isn't a dream I can ever embrace."

"Why not?" Annie asked, surprised. "Levi, that sounds like a wunderbaar dream. And you're well-read enough to write your own book. Have you even tried?"

"Nee, every time I put words to paper, I know my father would never approve," Levi sighed.

"Just like my mamm doesn't approve of the traveling library. Seems to me like you're preaching fate and faith and you're too afraid to follow your own advice. I believe in your dream, Levi, you should too." Annie smiled at him with affection. It was clear she had more confidence in him than Levi had ever had in himself.

Once again, she amazed him.

Perhaps he should pray to Gott for another miracle. A miracle for him and Annie to be together.

"I better go," Annie said with a sad smile. "If I get home too late, my mamm will have even more reason to complain. At least if I do my chores, she can't complain that the traveling library is keeping me from it."

Levi nodded. He knew Abram would be back soon, and his father would be up from his rest as well. "As always, it was gut to see you, Annie. Here are my books."

Levi handed her the books he had taken the week before. "My notes are in the front."

He didn't tell her he had addressed his notes to *my dearest Annie.*

"Denke. Here are my suggestions for this week. I left a note in each on why I recommend it," Annie said, handing him four books.

They said goodbye and Levi couldn't help but feel sad to see her go. Annie had become the highlight of his life and today, he had shared a secret with her he had never shared with anyone before.

He didn't know where he was going to find the time, but Annie was right. It was time he focused on chasing his own miracle—to write what was on his mind.

Chapter 8
Expectations &
Demands

"Aren't you going to singing?"

Annie turned to her mother with surprise in her eyes. "Nee, Mamm. I told you I don't want to go searching for love. You've heard what Amos said. Some of those girls at singing are so desperate they invite themselves for a buggy ride."

Rebecca clucked her tongue. "Ach, your bruder was exaggerating. Besides, I don't hear him complaining about taking another girl on a buggy ride every other Sunday."

Annie couldn't help but chuckle. "You're right, he isn't complaining at all."

"At least he's open to the thought of courting. He's a gut age too. A mann must start considering his options when he approaches his mid-twenties." Rebecca picked up her crotchet needle and threaded small circles as the beginning of something else.

"He'll make a gut husband and daed one day," Annie mused to herself. Her brother had teased her endlessly as a child, like any brother should, but she loved him with all her heart.

"Hardworking too. He'll make a great success of this farm when the time comes," Rebecca explained.

Annie knew her mother was referring to her father's will that hadn't been settled yet. Apparently, her father had a will drawn up with an Englisch lawyer in town and they were still waiting for the reading. According to her mother, the lawyer should contact them within the next few weeks. The stipulations of the will were weighing heavily on all their minds. As the son, it was only right that her brother inherited most of her father's assets.

"He'll need a gut wife to support him. Let's hope that sooner rather than later, the right girl goes on a buggy ride with him," Annie teased.

Her mother set down her crochet work and turned to Annie with a frown. "Just like you need a mann to support you. We can't expect your bruder to support you when he's married with a familye of his own."

The words were harsh and coldly spoken, making a tingle run down Annie's spine. "Mamm, Amos won't kick me to the fields when he finds someone he wants to spend his life with. Just like he won't put you out."

"That's the difference, Annie. We expect Amos to care for me in old age, unless you offer to. We expect you to find a mann to care for you. You won't find one prancing around the Englisch town and spending all your time on that buggy," Rebecca said sharply.

Annie suddenly wished she'd pretended to go to singing instead. As of late, every time she and her mother had a minute alone, her mother insisted on verbalizing her disapproval of the traveling library.

"Mamm, the traveling library was important to daed. Some people I see have no one else to talk to. Except for the books that bring them joy, Shakespeare and I also break the monotony of their quiet, often lonely lives. Doesn't that mean anything?" Annie tried to defend her position.

"Annie, it meant something. To your daed. He never intended for you to slave away behind the reins of a buggy," Rebecca argued.

"I still do my chores, and I'm home at a decent hour every day. Surely you can't fault me for that."

"Nee, I can't. But I can fault you for not being a proper frau. Men will notice and they will start looking past you to more suitable wives for the future. Before you know it, you'll be a spinster with nothing but books and an old horse for company. Is that what you really want?"

Annie sighed and shook her head. "Mamm, how can you make it sound as if I'm wasting my life away? I'm honoring Daed's memory. His life's work."

"You'll honor him more by finding a mann and starting a familye. The mann is the head of the haus, Annie. The way you're going on, you'll never have a haus, or a mann, only your own head to follow."

Annie understood the customs and the traditions. She understood they expected it of her to do the housekeeping chores and take care of her children one day, but did that mean that until that day arrived, she had to sit around waiting for the right man?

Or worse, search for him at singing.

All the men that attended their community's singings were related to her, already engaged, or simply too consumed with their own lives to even bother listening to her talk about books. Annie couldn't imagine spending her entire life with a man that didn't share her love for reading.

Levi came to mind and warmth spread through her chest. If only a man like Levi lived in their community. Then, without a doubt, Annie would have attended the singing.

"I'm still young, Mamm, there is still time," Annie tried to defend her position.

"Jah, but you're in your prime to have kinner. You're young and strong, you don't want to chase after toddlers when you're in your thirties," her mother warned.

Annie couldn't help but flash her mother a teasing smile. "Nee, I'll have my mann run after them instead while I do all the housekeeping chores and raise the other kinner."

"You can tease all you want, Annie Hauptfleisch, but you and I know that a traveling library isn't the answer for a young woman. It doesn't even bring you the slightest of income."

"It never brought Daed any income. He did to give back to the community," Annie argued.

"That might be, but we don't know what your daed's will says. If Amos inherits everything, you need to consider how you are going to make a living. Your daed might have inherited wealthily and we might have lived a comfortable life, but the will could change all that. What if he donated all the investments to libraries?"

Annie's face broadened with a smile. "I would admire him for it."

"And then how will we buy fruit, pantry staples, pay for the lamp oil and all the other expenses it takes to run a farm? These are things to consider. I honestly think that it's time for Shakespeare to retire and for you to act like the young eligible woman you are."

"You want me to stop the traveling library altogether?" Annie asked, horrified.

Her mother nodded firmly. "Jah, frankly, I'm tired of arguing about it. I think it's time your father's dream ends on a high note so that you can pursue your own dreams."

"What if Daed's dream *is* my dream?" Annie asked desperately.

"It shouldn't be. A young woman of your age should dream about having her own home, a family and a mann to care for," Rebecca said firmly.

"Mamm… please… Don't make me give up the traveling library…" Annie all but begged. "At least give me a month, six weeks to think about what you're asking. I'll need to warn the readers, I'll need to collect the books that have been borrowed…"

"Very well then… I'll give you a month, not a day more, to make sure word gets out and to collect all the outstanding books. But after that, it's over, Annie. Then you'll start attending singings and be the proper woman I raised you to be."

Tears burned Annie's eyes. She couldn't believe her mother was making her give up the traveling library. It was the only connection she still had to her father. Whether it was her anger or her grief, she wasn't sure, but she couldn't help but wonder if her mother wasn't jealous of the bond Annie had shared with her father.

Her mother had never enjoyed reading. It had been something that Annie, her father, had shared her entire life.

Regardless of her mother's reasons, Annie knew it would be hopeless to argue any further. Her mother was still the head of the home and regardless of that matter, Annie had to respect her.

She had never had any trouble with respecting her parents, her mother especially before, but now for the first time, she wondered if the bible meant you had to respect their decisions and demands regardless of whether you believed them to be wrong, or right?

Annie stood up, her heart heavy as she turned to her mother. "Jah, Mamm. Gut night."

Annie retreated to her bedroom and closed the door behind her. As soon as she was alone, she grabbed a book on the nightstand and held it to her chest before she allowed the tears to come.

No one would understand how heartbroken she felt, except for her father.

And perhaps a man that lived in the community on the other side of town.

Levi.

Chapter 9
Shooting Stars

"I see I'm not the only one struggling to sleep in this heat."

Levi turned at the sound of his brother's voice. "Among other things."

Abram took a seat beside Levi on the porch steps and yawned. "Funny thing is, I'm so tired it hurts, but every time I lie down it's as if a furnace lights up inside me and overcomes me with heat."

Levi chuckled. "I'll go fetch you a glass of cold water."

Levi returned to the porch with two glasses of water and sat down beside his brother. "Here you go."

"Denke," Abram said gratefully, and drank down the entire glass with only a few sips. "Why are you still awake?"

It might only be a little after ten pm, but usually most people in their community were asleep by eight pm. They retired early, because they rose just as early in the mornings.

"Just have some things on my mind," Levi said with a shrug.

"Does those *things* include the girl from the library buggy?" Abram teased and nudged him in the ribs with his elbow.

Levi shook his head indulgently at his brother's words. "Actually, it's something she said."

"Well, do I have to drag it from you, or are going to tell me?" Abram asked with a cocked brow.

"You know I like to read. Well… I've always thought about one day attempting my hand at writing. I never even considered really doing it until Annie encouraged me to."

Abram chuckled. "Daed's going to have a fit when he hears about this. He's already complaining about you reading all the time and now you want to write when you're not reading?"

Levi sighed and turned to his brother with a searching look. "You enjoy farming, don't you?"

"Jah, of course," Abram agreed.

"You enjoy the entire process; every moment's hard work right from when we plow until we harvest the last row. You've always enjoyed it, and you're gut at it."

Abram looked chuffed with the compliment.

"Can you imagine if someone told you you couldn't farm? Could you imagine what it would feel like if you're told to spend the rest of your life doing something that doesn't make you as happy?"

"What are you saying, Levi?" Abram asked carefully. "Doesn't farming make you happy?"

"I do it because I have to, Abram, not because I enjoy it like you do. I just think… never mind. Daed will never understand."

"I can't imagine someone telling me I'm not allowed to farm. It would be like a punishment. If that's really how you feel about farming, Levi, then you should do what Annie said. Try your hand at writing."

"Daed insists I have to take over the farm one day–how can I when I know I won't enjoy it?" Levi asked his brother with a curious look. "I'm not like you Abram. You have dirt running through your veins. Daed just thinks I don't like the hard work. It's not that at all. I don't mind the work, I just don't…"

"You just don't see yourself doing it for the rest of your life?" Abram asked carefully.

Levi nodded. "It doesn't matter. Daed will never understand. As the eldest, I'm expected to take over the farm and to continue the heritage of those that farmed this land before us."

Abram laid a hand on his brother's shoulder and smiled. "You know, a wise bruder once told me that when we don't find the answers we're looking for, we need to pray harder."

Levi laughed, feeling peace and calm wash over him. He and Abram had always been good friends, but it was times like now that he was reminded how blessed he was to have a brother. "I'll do just that. I think I'll try to sleep now."

"Jah, me too. Tomorrow morning Daed will scold us for being up at all hours of the night," Abram agreed.

Levi headed to his room and closed the door behind him. He opened the windows to let in the cool evening air. There by the window, he stood and looked out into the night sky as he prayed.

"Gott, please hear my prayers tonight. Please help me find joy and please my daed at the same time. My whole life he's been telling me I have to become the next Hertzler farmer on this land, and yet I can't seem to gather any excitement at the thought. All I can think about is that I enjoy books more. Is that wrong? I need to put my words on paper, to bring the written word to others and yet I'm afraid that if I pursue that need, it will harm my relationship with my father.

Please help me Gott.

Help Annie, who might have to give up the traveling library, something that brings her so much pleasure Gott. Denke for bringing her into my life and for the opportunity to become her friend.

Gott, please guide us, guide us in the direction you want our lives to lead. Guide us toward joy and happiness and most of all, help us cherish our faith always.

I ask this not because I am deserving Gott, because I know only a wise sheep herder will herd his flock to fresh water. Amen."

Levi watched a star shoot across the sky and felt a smile curve his mouth. His prayers might not have been answered, but he had a gut feeling they had been heard.

Chapter 10
A Gift Horse

Annie's mother had been quiet over the last few days about her giving up on the traveling library, but Annie knew that didn't mean she wasn't still against it.

Every morning Annie climbed onto the buggy, she wondered if it would be her last.

She had taken special care to wear gloves whenever she held the reins, to give her mother one less thing to complain about, but Annie knew it wasn't about the callouses, the gloves, or even the long hours on the road.

Her mother was concerned for her safety, especially because Annie visited with members of the other community that her mother didn't know. Deep down, Annie understood her mother's reticence, but she couldn't help but feel that if her mother joined her just once, she would understand why Annie didn't want to give up on her father's dream.

She pushed the thoughts of her mother and the end drawing closer for the traveling library out of her mind and instead thought of her next stop. She had gone through special trouble to procure a book on fiction writing for Levi.

When her mother had sent her to the Saturday market in town to stock up on fresh vegetables and fruit, Annie had stopped by the small bookstore in town and found a second-hand copy of a book that would help Levi write his first book.

Her heart swelled with excitement. She knew in her mind that Levi would be a skilled writer. He had a wonderful mind, and she knew readers would appreciate it just as much as she did.

It was a little before lunchtime when she turned into the Hertzler yard. At the sight of Levi's father sitting on the porch, Annie waved to him with a smile before she stopped the buggy under the tree for Shakespeare to quench his thirst.

Annie considered walking towards the porch, but she was a little apprehensive from the look in Isaac's gaze. Levi's father wasn't happy about her stopping by. Had something happened she didn't know of? Or was her timing just off today?

Perhaps Levi had something to do, and she was interrupting his work?

"Annie!" Levi called out, coming out of the house with his books under his arm. He glanced briefly at his father before he jogged down the stairs and crossed the yard to her. "You're early today."

"I know," Annie said guiltily. "Is that a problem?"

"Nee, nee of course not," Levi said easily as he handed her the books he had borrowed the last time.

"Your father doesn't seem to agree," Annie said quietly, feeling Isaac's scouring gaze on her and Shakespeare.

Levi sighed with an apology in his eyes. "My daed doesn't understand my love for reading… I don't think he ever will. He's not mad at you. He's agitated with me."

Annie nodded, although that didn't stop her from squirming beneath Isaac's hard gaze. "I brought you something I think you might enjoy."

"New words for a hungry mind. I always enjoy your suggestions," Levi said with a warm smile.

Annie couldn't help but feel her heart swell with affection. Over the last month, she and Levi had become more than just book friends. It felt as if they had become real friends as well. "Well, today I don't have fiction for you. I have a different type of self-help book."

Levi frowned with curiosity. "Really? Well then, show it to me."

Annie reached onto the seat of the buggy and pulled out the three books she had set aside for Levi. "The first is my favorite Christian inspirational romance, the second is a book about man overcoming impossible challenges and the third...." Annie handed him the third book. "Is a book about how to go about writing your first novel."

Levi stared down at the book with a smile that spoke of gratitude and appreciation. "Annie, this is..."

"Just what you need to get started on your great Amish novel. And it's yours. It's not part of the library," Annie replied with a smile.

"Nee, it's more than that. It's... it's the most thoughtful gift anyone has ever given me. It... Denke," Levi finally finished, clearly at a loss for words.

Their gazes met and if Annie had any doubts about the feelings she had developed for Levi, she confirmed them now in her mind. She didn't feel like a friend when Levi looked at her, and she didn't think of him as a friend either.

Although it was impossible, she couldn't stop herself from dreaming of a world without obstacles. A world where she could drive the library buggy with Levi at her side. A world where their parents and their expectations didn't hold them back from following their dreams.

Levi reached for her hand and shook his head. "You're the most wunderbaar person I've ever met, do you know that?"

Annie blushed slightly. "I feel the same about you."

Their gazes held for a few more seconds. So many words going unsaid and yet there was so much more Annie still wanted to say when Levi finally broke away. "I have to get back to work, but Annie…"

"I know. You're grateful and you appreciate it. I was hoping you would feel that way."

"Has your mamm said anything more about putting an end to the library buggy?" Levi asked, concerned.

Annie shook her head. "She hasn't said another word about it yet. But she is still thinking about it, I can tell. We're to meet with daed's lawyers later this week. Then we'll finally know what's to come of the library."

"I'll pray for a miracle Annie. So many people rely on you and these books," Levi said with a warm smile. "I'll see you next week."

With that, Levi turned and jogged towards the porch. His father stood there and watched Annie with an eagle eye. Annie had never felt unwelcome on the Hertzler farm…

Until today.

She climbed into the buggy and took Shakespeare's reins. As she directed him out of the yard, she wondered if she should be more worried about her mother wanting the traveling library to stop, or the look in Isaac Hertzler's gaze.

She prayed for both matters.

Chapter 11
Ironclad & Generous

Annie glanced at her mother and her brother and couldn't help but feel anxious about what they were about to hear.

The lawyer had stopped by the house three days ago to notify them that her father's estate had been finalized. He had invited them to come to his office for a meeting to learn the stipulations of her father's will.

Ever since the lawyer had stopped by the house, there had been a dark cloud sucking the light out of their home. It was as if the whole family felt anxious to know what would come of her father's fortune.

The fortune that had supported them their whole lives.

Just like Annie, her mother was concerned that their lives would irrevocably change after this meeting. Josef Hauptfleisch had been an honourable man, but often his heart had spoken louder than his common sense.

It was a general feeling amongst Annie, her mother, and her brother that her father might just have given all of his fortune to charity. Her father had always felt privileged to have inherited wealthy and at times, Annie could tell he even felt guilty.

Would that guilt have driven him to take that privilege away from his family after his death?

"Well then, I see everyone is here. Do you have questions before I begin?"

The lawyer, a Mr. Thompson, glanced at them as he sat down behind his desk.

Annie's mother cleared her throat. "I guess, we're all just curious that if we don't agree with the terms of my mann's will, if it can be changed?"

Mr. Thompson shook his head. "Unfortunately, Mr. Hauptfleisch created an ironclad will that didn't allow for any changes. For the last fifteen years, we've had a standing appointment every March to go over the terms. Which means, this will was revised only month's before his passing. He was sound of mind and signed it in my presence. No changes can be entered into hereafter."

Annie swallowed with a nod, even as her mother accepted the lawyer's words.

"Shall we begin?" the lawyer asked.

"Jah, please. I need to get back to the farm," Amos said, glancing at the clock on the wall.

"Right, then I'll begin with you," Mr. Thompson said, looking right at Amos. "Your father's will determines that you inherit the farm, all the outbuildings and the house. There is a large sum of money that he left you, with the only condition to build a dawdi haus for your mother to stay in for as long as she is willing."

Amos nodded, clearly relieved that the farm, his livelihood and passion, wasn't taken away from him. He turned to his mother with a broad smile. "I'll build you the best dawdi house you've ever seen, Mamm."

Rebecca smiled gratefully at her son before she turned back to the lawyer.

Mr. Thompson continued. "Annie, his daughter that shared his love for reading, inherits the traveling library, all the books in the library and a wealthy sum of money that will make sure that she never wants for anything. It is his request that you continue with his route and serve his readers like he did all these years."

Annie felt relief wash over her along with gratitude even as her mother gasped beside her.

"Surely that's not appropriate! For a young girl to travel the back roads on her own every day...." Rebecca cried out in anger.

"Like I said, Mrs. Hauptfleisch, the will is iron-clad and these stipulations can't be changed," Mr. Thompson said easily before he continued. "Rebecca Hauptfleisch, to you he left an account with enough funds to make sure you are comfortable and cared for. He also bequeathed you with the authority to choose which charities to donate the balance of his investments to."

Annie turned to her mother, who had turned as pale as a sheet. "There is still money left?"

"Yes, indeed there is. Your husband was very careful about his expenditures over the years and made a few very lucrative investments. He left me a list of charities he would like to support, but the final decision remains in your hands."

"Which charities?" Rebecca asked, shocked, still reeling from the information she had just received.

"There is a charity that supports the distribution of books in third world countries, the Red Cross, a few missionary churches across the country, and then there is the community fund in your ordnung."

"How much is left?" Amos asked curiously as he leaned forward in his chair.

Annie's eyes widened with shock when the lawyer mentioned an amount that had too many zeros for Annie to remember. "Mamm, with that you could donate to all the charities Daed mentioned."

"I... I need a few days to think about this," Rebecca said, reaching for her purse. "Denke for your time."

Annie and Amos followed their mother outside. Once they were seated in the buggy, Amos laughed. "Daed was truly a wunderbaar mann. Not only did he make sure that Annie and I can continue living our dreams, but he ensured that all of us are taken care of for the foreseeable future. And the money that's left... Mamm did you know about it?"

Rebecca shook her head. "I knew your daed inherited wealthily. I also knew that when he sold the other farms, he wanted to invest the money because we didn't need it. I never for one moment thought.... It's a lot of money."

"You can bless many people with it, Mamm. Daed was a very generous mann, I think he'll support whatever decision you make, just to know the money is going to a gut cause," Annie said, reaching for her mother's hand.

Rebecca's hand was shaking from the shock, but Annie just held it tighter. She turned to Annie with a sad smile. "I'm sorry I gave you so much trouble about the traveling library. I guess now I have to accept it's what your daed wanted for you."

"It's what I want for myself," Annie smiled warmly. "I promise I'll be careful, Mamm." Annie turned to her brother with a curious look. "The will makes provision for Mamm living in the dawdi haus. Does that mean you're kicking me out?"

Amos laughed as he took the reins. "I guess you can stay until you find a mann."

"That will not happen any time soon," Rebecca said with a sigh.

"Then I'll just put you up in the dawdi haus with Mamm. A newly married man needs his privacy," Amos teased.

Annie's eyes widened. "A newly married man. Does that mean you have a sweetheart?"

"For some time, jah, I just wanted to be sure before I told you about it. But now that I know my future is on the farm, I don't see any reason to put off our engagement for another day. If I have your blessing, Mamm, I'd like to ask for her hand in marriage."

Rebecca's smile lit up. Annie could see that Amos's news made her mother completely forget about the traveling library and the charities she had to choose. "Of course, I'm so happy for you, Amos. I wish you the type of marriage and friendship your daed and I shared for so many years."

"I do too," Amos agreed.

"Now we just have to find your schweschder a mann," Rebecca added, turning to Annie.

For a moment, Annie wanted to tell her mother she had already found him, but she kept quiet. She wasn't certain if

Levi shared her feelings and the last thing she wanted to do was to get her mother's hopes up, only to let her down later.

Chapter 12
When the Cub Threatens the Lion

As sleep gave way to wakefulness, Levi realized something was wrong. There was light streaming into his room, the room hot and muggy. He lay back and stretched as a yawn escaped him.

Closing his eyes to rest them for just a minute longer, he promised that last night was the last time he allowed himself to write into the early morning hours.

He hadn't thought that he would become so enamored with his own writing, but once he had picked up a pen and began to write, he lost himself more and more in the story. During the day, he worked in the fields and at night, as soon as everyone retired to their rooms, he burned to put more words on paper. His book was coming along faster than he expected and he was enjoying every second of writing.

The only problem was he wasn't getting much sleep.

He opened his eyes and glanced at the bedside clock. A frown creased his brow as he reached for the clock. He shook it to make sure it was working, only to hear the soft mechanical ticking.

Levi threw back the covers and jumped out of bed. He was dressed within seconds and rushing towards the kitchen. He had overslept by fifteen minutes a few days ago, but this morning it had been much over fifteen minutes.

His father would be waiting for him.

As soon as he stepped into the kitchen, he saw his father sitting by the table waiting for him with a cocked brow. "I hope it was a gut book?"

Levi dragged a hand through his hair before he reached for his wide brim hat that hung behind the door. "Jah, I'm sorry I overslept."

"You didn't oversleep, Levi. You simply failed to get up at all. It's almost noon and you expect me to just accept it? I have one son slaving away in the fields on a hot day and another who prefers to spend his nights with books and to leave the hard work to others," Isaac began in a voice that Levi knew suggested nothing good.

"It's not like that, Daed. I'm really sorry. Why didn't you wake me?" Levi asked, exasperated. To oversleep by six hours was unheard of. Especially in a community that started the day before six am.

"Because I am not your keeper. Because you are a grown man. You should be aware of the consequences of your actions. Isaac slammed his fist on the table. "Your mamm urged me to be patient with you. She begged me to humor your love for the written word and I have. Heaven knows I have. I've let that buggy stop by for years. I've allowed you to fuss over books and talk about them until none of us were interested to hear. I've had to listen to you carry on about dinosaurs, insects, and poems written by dead men, but that's enough!" Isaac cried out with so much venom in his voice that Levi actually took a step back.

"Daed, I'm sorry. It won't ever happen again. I'll work until midnight if I have to. You won't have to worry about me not doing my part."

"Your part? I don't care about your *part!* The only thing you care about is books, that's what I care about. I'm done, Levi. I'm done. I'm glad you say that the book you read last night was a gut one, because it was your last. You can leave your books in the entry hall; I'll return them to *that* girl when she comes again. I will no longer let your bad habits affect this farm. Is that clear?" Isaac asked in a threatening tone.

Levi wanted to plead with his father. He wanted to beg for his father to understand. To at least sympathize that Levi didn't mean to sleep late. But in the current mood his father was in, it was clear, nothing Levi said now would change his mind.

His days of reading were over. "Jah, Daed. You've made yourself clear."

Levi collected the books and placed them in the entry hall. He hadn't even had a chance to write Annie a note yet. Instead, he quickly scribbled a note with his address on it and asked her to write him.

He didn't bother with coffee or grabbing something to eat, instead he made his way to the fields where Abram was working.

"That bad?" Abram asked when Levi reached him.

"Worse. I'm sorry I let you down. You should've woken me," Levi said apologetically.

"I can manage these fields fairly well on my own. Besides, I wanted to wake you. Daed insisted you be left."

Levi shook his head, feeling angry with his father. It was as if his father had ambushed him into taking his books away. As if he had planned an attack which would leave Levi defenseless.

"Did you write last night?" Abram asked, tugging out a weed. "I saw your lamp was still on after midnight. Or were you reading?"

Levi knew it no longer mattered, but he nodded. "I was writing. I began ten days ago, and so far, at least he can't take that from me."

"Make sure he doesn't find out, then. Before you know it, he'll be hiding all the paper and pens in the house as well," Abram warned.

Levi knew his brother was right. "He also said Annie can't stop by anymore. No more traveling library."

Abram frowned and glanced at his brother with sympathy in his eyes. "I'm so sorry, bruder. I know she meant more to you than the books she gave you access to."

"Jah," Levi admitted heavily. "Now I'll never see her again. If I wasn't of sound mind, I might have considered running away."

Abram chuckled. "And what gut would that do? You're too honest, you'll be consumed by the guilt."

"And now… now I'm consumed by anger and regret," Levi pointed out.

"Just give him time, bruder. He'll come to his senses. If not, I'll try to talk some sense into him. He can't discourage your reading just because he doesn't understand it."

"If only I was more like you," Levi said with a heavy sigh.

"Well, he's watching from the porch. So for today, at least try to do exactly what I do," Abram warned.

Levi nodded and helped his brother weed between the rows of corn. He respected his brother's love for the land and farming, but he wondered if his brother even understood why the corn needed to be weeded.

Did his brother know weeds lure pests? Did he know that if weeds constricted the roots of the corn it would influence their harvest?

Did Abram even care?

It was as if his whole family just did what they were told, what their ancestors did before them, without even understanding why.

Was it so wrong of Levi that he wanted to know the why behind every action taken? That he wanted to know the consequences of not doing what they were *told* to do? He tugged out a weed and realized that the consequences of writing into the morning hours hadn't just cost him his friendship, and possible relationship with Annie.

It had cost him his love for reading.

What else would his father insist on taking from him before he realized Levi wasn't the son that wanted to take over the farm?

What was wrong with allowing Abram to farm and giving Levi enough freedom to pursue a life of his own? Not even a life outside the community, just perhaps a job where he could be with books.

Would it be so wrong if he wanted to work in a bookstore, for example?

He only had to glance towards the porch to know his father would never accept or bless any job that involved books. In his father's eyes, books were a distraction, unnecessary information that corrupted the mind.

But what his father didn't know was that books were so much more.

They were a way of sharing knowledge, of renewing your faith, and most of all, they were a way to find a brief escape from the monotony of everyday life.

"Why do you think he doesn't want me to read? I've already been baptized, Abram. It's not like it can corrupt me to leave the community to live with the Englisch."

Abram turned to him with a crooked smile and a shake of his head. "You don't know, do you? Or if you know you've never realized it."

"Realized what?"

"Ever since we were born, Daed was the wisest, strongest, and most respectable mann we knew. We admired him, because he always had the answers."

"Jah, rightfully so," Levi agreed.

"That's changed over the last few years, Levi. When someone wants advice, they ask you. When I need to know something about the soil, the pests, or even how to maximize the crops, I ask you. You've taken over his position as the wisest man in the house. I might be wrong, but I think he feels that you've replaced him."

"What? That isn't true!" Levi argued.

"Nee, it isn't. But he feels his knowledge is inferior to yours and every time you read another book, you become a little wiser."

"So, should I act dumb?" Levi huffed impatiently.

"Nee, just perhaps stop telling him how much you know," Abram suggested.

Levi couldn't believe what his brother was saying, but it made sense. His knowledge threatened his father, especially because his father didn't have access to a traveling library when he was young.

For a moment he sympathized, but then the anger returned.

Just because his father felt threatened, didn't mean he had to punish Levi for learning more than he ever had.

Chapter 13
A Cold Goodbye

Annie had been counting the days until she could see Levi again. Ever since the reading of her father's will, she couldn't wait to tell Levi that the future of the traveling library had been secured. She knew he had been praying for her and she wanted to thank him.

But aside from sharing all the exciting news in her father's will, she wanted to see Levi again. He had become the person she wanted to share her news with. The person she looked forward to seeing, and above all that, the one person who could make her smile without even trying.

Over the last few days, she could positively feel the change in her mother's demeanor since the reading of the will. They no longer wondered what was going to happen. They finally had the answers they had been waiting for.

Amos was excited about officially taking over the farm and her mother was more at ease with her father's decision about the traveling library. It was as if her mother had made peace that this was what her father had wanted and what Annie wanted for herself. She no longer discouraged Annie or made her feel guilty, instead she greeted her with a basket of fruit for the road and a warm smile.

It was as if everything was finally falling into place. After her father's death, she had felt so lost and uncertain about her future and the future of the traveling library, but now she could move ahead with peace in her heart.

As she made her way through the town of Old Apple, excitement mounted. She couldn't wait to share her news with Levi. She also couldn't wait to ask him if he'd given any more thought to writing a book of his own. She knew he had the talent and the imagination. She truly hoped he'd give himself a chance.

Anni believed in Levi, just like he had believed in her.

Her heart fluttered with joy when Levi's home came into view. She wondered if he had made them sun tea again. Would they sit under the tree and talk for a while? Talking to Levi had truly become the best part of her week.

As she guided Shakespeare into the yard, Annie knew instantly something was wrong. The water trough hadn't been filled for Shakespeare. A frowned creased her brow, finding it strange. Levi always made sure there was fresh water for Shakespeare.

Perhaps he'd just forgotten, she assured herself before she stopped in front of the barn. She climbed off and glanced around, but there wasn't sight of Levi anywhere. She walked around the barn and could see him working in the fields with his brother. A smile curved her mouth as she held up her hand and waved to him. "Hullo!"

Levi barely glanced up; he didn't even bother to wave. Instead, he turned his back on her and continued to work.

Annie wasn't sure what she had done or said that had upset him, but she couldn't understand why he was being so rude? She stood there for a moment contemplating walking over to him in the field before she decided against it.

Just as she was about to call out to him again, she heard Isaac Hertzler's voice behind her.

"Miss Hauptfleisch?"

Annie turned to see Mr. Hertzler, standing a few feet from the porch. "Guten Mayrie Mr. Hertzler. How are you this morning?"

He shrugged, barely giving anything away. "Here, Levi won't be needing these anymore. Neither will he be needing the services of the traveling library…. Ever again."

"But… Levi loves to read. I'm sorry I don't understand?" Annie asked, but Mr. Hertzler gave her a grim look.

"I'm sure I made myself clear, Miss Hauptfleisch. Now, I'll appreciate it if you would leave my property."

His voice was hard and cold, almost frightening as he looked at Annie through his narrowed eyes. Annie opened her mouth to plea on Levi's behalf but knew it wouldn't be any use.

Instead, she nodded and ambled back to the buggy. She climbed in and took the reins before talking to Shakespeare. "We'll have to get you a drink of water at the Widow Baker's."

Shakespeare let out a loud whinny, as if it also disappointed him that they weren't staying for a visit.

Annie glance at the books Levi had and felt her heart break in two. Would she ever talk to him again? See him again?

She turned onto the dirt road and noticed a piece of paper slip from the cover of the book right on the top.

Reaching for it, she was relieved to see it was a note from Levi.

But this note didn't have his usual thoughts on the books he had read, instead it was short and very concise. Judging by his writing in the past, it was clear he'd been in a hurry when he'd written this note.

My dearest Annie,

I'm not allowed to read anymore. My daed forbids me. I'll try to explain everything later, but for now, just know this; not reading and not being able to see you is breaking my heart. Please write to me, at least that way I won't lose you completely.

Levi

A tear slipped over cheek when she imagined how hard it must be for Levi not to read. But even worse, not even be able to talk to her. She felt as if she had been bereft of something that had never really been hers and yet, just reading his words made her feel as if she hadn't lost everything.

He cared.

She wasn't sure how much, but he cared.

She wouldn't delay another day, she promised herself. As soon as she arrived home this evening, he would write to Levi. If they couldn't talk in person, she could at least talk to him in her letters. She could reveal her good news and even share her latest thoughts on the books she had read this week.

Chapter 14
Intercepted Mail

After four long days in the field, Levi was tired.

Not because of the hard work or the harsh sun, because it felt as if his soul remained hungry. The work kept his hands busy, but not his mind.

He spent his evenings writing in secret and when he wasn't writing, he was thinking about Annie. But he still felt that hollowness in his soul without having books to turn to for knowledge or solace. It was a feeling he couldn't explain to anyone in his family, but he knew Annie would understand.

He had prayed that his father wouldn't find the note he had snuck into the books for Annie, because at least if she had received that letter, she would know he wasn't rude by choice.

Levi and his family ate dinner in silence, just like they had for the last few nights. Although Abram hadn't voiced his opinion on his father's actions, his silence made Levi feel like he had an ally. It might be a silent ally, but at least he had an ally.

Although it didn't seem to affect his father at all.

Once they had finished eating, Abram cleared the dishes.

Isaac turned to Levi with a determined look. "I can see you've worked hard these last few days Levi. You've taken responsibility and I'm glad for it. When a man works hard during the day, he doesn't have time to waste on books at night."

Levi clenched his jaw. If only his father knew he wasn't wasting his time on reading books at night, he was actually writing one. But just like Abram had warned him, he remained mute. The last thing he needed was for his father to hide all the pens and paper in the house as well.

"When you take over the farm, this is what your life is going to be like. You will have a familye to support, a frau to do the chores around the house and a farm that will provide for you, just like many generations of Hertzlers have done before you. There is no shame in hard work," Isaac reiterated.

"I don't mind the hard work," Levi said flatly.

"That's gut, because you need to be focused on your future. You need to court and move ahead in life. Books have held you back for too long."

"Books have never held me back, Daed. They only contributed to the person I am today," Levi said stubbornly.

As soon as the words left his mouth, Abram cleared his throat, as if warning him to keep quiet rather than upset his father even more.

"I'm just glad you won't be wasting any more time on books. I know you blame me for making this decision, but it's the right one," Isaac said firmly before he stood up. "I'm going to turn in."

Levi let out a sigh as soon as his father's footsteps faded out of earshot. "I swear this is a punishment worse than slavery...."

Abram turned to him with an understanding look. "Patience, bruder. Patience."

"Why doesn't he just give you the farm? Why do I have to take it? You enjoy farming. But just because the eldest son has always inherited the land, I have to."

"Daed is strict with tradition, Levi, regardless of what we think of it," Abram said heavily.

For the first time, Levi realized that his father's stubborn decision wasn't only affecting him, but it was affecting Abram as well. "I'm sorry Abram, I didn't even realize how hard this must be on you."

"I'll make my own way. That's what the second son does. But here, I found it in the mailbox today, thought it was better if Daed didn't see it." Abram handed him an envelope.

Levi's heart skipped a beat as he recognized Annie's handwriting. "It came today?"

"Jah, this morning," Abram smiled at him with a teasing grin. I guess you won't be writing tonight will you, you'll be reading instead."

Levi chuckled. "Who knows, I might just write back."

My dearest Levi

I was so sorry to learn of your daed's cruel decision to forbid books. I assure you I will try and keep your eager mind fed with notes from stories I've read.

I was so disappointed that I couldn't see you. I have the best news in the world that I wanted to share with you.

My daed's will has been finalized and, along with a handsome sum of money, it was his will for me to inherit the traveling library and continue with his route.

My mamm has not once mentioned stopping it again. I so looked forward to telling you all this in person. But I guess it would have to wait for another day.

I hope that you have taken this time to search inside yourself for the book I know you can write. I know it must be hard for you not to read, but Levi, I believe in you.

Please believe in yourself and follow your dreams.

I'll keep you in my prayers and pray every day that your daed comes to see reason in his unfair ruling.

Regards,

Annie

P.S. Below are my notes on some of Shakespeare's classics and a recent Christian inspirational book I read.

By the time Levi reached the end of Annie's letter, he was smiling from ear to ear. It overjoyed him to learn that Annie could continue with the library buggy, and more than anything he was happy that it had been her father's wish for her all along.

Miracles do still happen, he decided.

He wasn't sure one was in the cards for him, though. He had a feeling it would take more than a miracle for his father to see reason in allowing books under his roof again.

Levi pushed the sad thoughts aside and instead focused on writing Annie a cheerful letter.

Chapter 15
A Gift That Can Be Tamed

Annie woke to the sound of hammering and pounding.

A frown creased her brow as she stood up and moved to the window to see what all the commotion was. As soon as she drew back the curtains, a smile curved her mouth.

The lumber had arrived yesterday and today, Amos was officially building her mother's dawdi haus. It was going to take him a long time to do everything himself and only when he wasn't busy on the farm, but he insisted he didn't want someone else to do it.

She knew that for Amos, building the dawdi haus himself was his way of making the farm his own. He had drawn up the plans, he had set out the perfect spot, and most of all, he had consulted with their mother every single step of the way.

Usually a dawdi haus was only one bedroom, a small kitchen, and a living room, but Amos had taken it to the next level.

The dawdi haus he was building for their mother would have two bedrooms, a kitchen, a mud room, a small living room, and a porch for her to watch the sunset from.

Although Annie had only seen the plans a friend of Amos's had drawn, she knew it was going to be perfect.

She changed and headed to the kitchen, only to find her mother standing at the window watching Amos work.

"Guten Mayrie Mamm," Annie greeted her mother with a smile.

"Morning, Annie," Rebecca said briefly over her shoulder. "I really don't know why he insists on building it himself. It's too much work. We have the money to hire a carpenter, and yet he refuses to even consider hiring one."

"Mamm, leave him be. I think he wants to do it himself, or at least start it by himself. Just like every single other Hauptfleisch mann that has ever inherited this property, Amos wants to make it his own. He wants to do something that puts his mark on it, if that makes sense."

"Fine, he designed it, he chose the spot... he's made his mark. Can't he hire someone now?"

Annie laughed. "Give it time, Mamm. As soon as he realizes he can't handle the dawdi haus construction and the farm, he'll give in. But it has to be his decision to make."

"Jah, jah. Ach, I forgot yesterday. This came for you in the mail." Rebecca handed Annie a thick envelope. "I do not know what it is, but it's quite the package."

Annie smiled gratefully when she noticed the post mark and the handwriting. "I know exactly who it's from."

After enjoying a quick breakfast and drinking her coffee at lightning speed, Annie retreated to her bedroom to open Levi's letter. It had been more than a week since she'd written him and she'd almost thought that he wasn't ever going to write her.

To now hold his letter in her hands, and such a thick one at that, made her heart swell with hope and joy.

My dearest Annie

I was overjoyed to learn about your news. I am so glad that although I won't be able to share in the wonderful world of books you bring to the doorstep of so many people, others will continue to enjoy it for years to come.

I'm glad that your father's will has been finalized and that you now feel more prepared for the future.

I have little news, no books to tell you about or interesting tales about working in the fields, but I do have something else I'd like to share with you.

Ever since my daed forbade books, I've slowly begun to write. At first it felt foolish and as if I was simply putting gibberish down on paper, but with every page I finished, I became more and more invested in the story.

Although my bruder Abram knows that I'm writing, you're the only person I'm willing to share it with. Please don't hesitate to be brutally honest. If you don't think it carries any merit, please tell me. I'd rather learn from you that I have no talent and should dedicate my life to the work of a farmer, than to learn it from someone else.

I miss you, Annie.

Not just the books, but our visits.

I know it's probably not appropriate for me to say this, but I looked forward to seeing you each week. You were the first person who understood my love for reading, the first to encourage me to write. I will forever be grateful to you for that.

Love,
Levi

Annie read over his sign off again and again to make sure her eyes weren't deceiving her. Instead of signing off with his usual *regards,* Levi had signed off with the word *love.*

Her heart skipped a beat, wondering if she should be as bold next time and do the same. She reached for the pages behind the letter and soon found herself lost in an Amish romance. The more she read, the more she realized the story Levi was telling was their story.

A story of two kindred souls living in opposite communities that form a friendship through their love for books. By the time Annie reached the last page, she knew two things without a doubt.

Levi did like her in *that* way.

And Levi had more talent than she had ever imagined.

He hadn't finished the book just yet, but Annie already knew that what she held in her hands would be more than enough to put out a few feelers.

Tomorrow she wouldn't be taking the traveling buggy on its route. Instead, tomorrow she would spend her day at the library.

Chapter 16
A Stranger in Danger

"The corn harvest is looking gut so far," Isaac commented as Abram and Levi sat down at the table for lunch.

"Jah, the rain has been kind to us and Levi's advice about the weed control has really helped deter pests in the cornfields," Abram said with a smile for Levi.

Levi shrugged. Although he was glad for his family that the corn harvest promised to be a good one, he couldn't seem to summon the same excitement as his family. He enjoyed the hard work, but he plotted the next chapter of his book while he worked, instead of thinking about how wonderful the harvest would be.

"See, I told you, you'll soon come to love farming and forget about those ridiculous books," Isaac said triumphantly.

"Are you expecting company, Daed?" Abram asked, glancing out the window as an Englisch car pulled into the drive.

"Nee, who would I know with a car?" Isaac grunted.

Both Isaac and Abram turned to Levi with a questioning look.

"Don't look at me, I don't know who that is," Levi said with a shrug before taking another bite of his sandwich.

Silence hung over the kitchen for a few moments, until there was a knock on the door.

Abram stood up. "Probably just got lost."

He headed to the door and from the kitchen Levi could hear muted conversation until footsteps moved towards the kitchen.

"Levi, this mann says he's looking for you," Abram said with a curious look.

Levi frowned, not recognizing the Englischer in the suit at all. "I'm sorry, do I know you?"

"No, no, not at all. But it's such a pleasure to meet you, Mr. Hertzler. Your mind is fascinating and I can't wait to discuss this manuscript with you." The man held out a hand. "I'm sorry. It seems I forgot my manners. I'm Andy Johnson with the Purple Owl publishing Group."

Levi felt his heart race as he realized this man had read the chapters he had written. He quickly put two and two together and realized that Annie must have sent them to him.

"I uhm…." Surprised and not knowing what else to do. Levi stood up and shook the man's hand. "It's gut to meet you."

"Wonderful." Mr. Johnson pulled out a chair and took a seat at the table, as if he was a regular guest. After introducing himself to Abram and Levi's father, he pulled out the chapters Levi had written by hand.

"I was very surprised to receive these chapters. I can't remember the last time I received a submission written by hand. But I must say Mr. Hertzler, your work is of the highest quality. It's inspiring, honest, and most of all, it draws the reader in to experience every emotion and every scene. It's going to make a bestseller, that's why I'm here," Mr. Johnson continued with excitement.

"I'm sorry, are you saying Levi *wrote* those?" Isaac asked through clenched teeth.

"Yes, yes, I am. Your son has a rare talent, Mr. Hertzler. A talent that could make him a very wealthy and famous man. I would love to represent him and bring this book to the world of publishing."

"When did you write that?" Isaac demanded, slamming his fist on the table with such force that the Englischer all but jumped.

"At night… when I had the time. When you told me I couldn't read, I began to write," Levi answered honestly.

"I told you—NO MORE BOOKS!" Isaac cried out.

"I'm sorry. I don't mean to cause any trouble. I just thought that Mr. Hertzler, Levi, would be interested in having his work published, if I was wrong…" Mr. Johnson backed away from the enemy lines with such grace that Levi wondered if he was going to run at any moment.

"He's not interested. I think you've wasted enough of our time, Mr. Johnson; we have a farm to tend to," Isaac said, standing up. He made it very clear their meeting was over and that Mr. Johnson was no longer welcome.

Mr. Johnson glanced at Levi with sympathy in his eyes. "Is this true that you're not interested?"

"I already answered. Now, leave. And never impose on my hospitality again. You and your book-lover kind are not welcome here. Not now, never!"

Mr. Johnson gathered his things, and all but ran for the door.

Levi hung his head in both shame and regret. For just a minute, he had hoped his father would be proud of him. For a few seconds, he thought his father would understand how much the written word meant to him, instead he had only been embarrassed and now his father would make sure he would never write again.

His heart clenched in his chest; his appetite gone.

He wished he could talk to Annie and thank her for going through the trouble of sending out his work. He never thought his midnight writing would amount to anything. Although it still didn't, it made him feel a little better to know that at least his writing was good.

Annie would understand that.

Annie was the only person who supported his dream.

His father was the only person standing in the way of it.

He found himself caught between the two poles of a magnet. On the one side there was Annie and the life of a writer he dreamed of and on the other there was life on the farm, with his father to answer to and endless days in the sun with no mental stimulation at all.

"That was the last time I heard about books, writing, or talent — you hear me! Now get back to the fields and start doing the work that is expected of you." His father's tone was quiet, but it held every threat Levi could imagine.

Levi stood up and walked out of the kitchen, already knowing that before nightfall, his father would've commandeered the rest of the chapters he had written as well as all his writing supplies.

Annie might have thought she was helping. It would shatter her if she knew that her help had just cost him the ability to write as well.

Chapter 17
Shine Your Light

After hearing from Mr. Johnson about how he was going to see Levi and offer him a publishing deal, Annie couldn't wait to read his letter. She gratefully accepted it from the mail man before she rushed to her room and tore open the envelope. But soon, tears were rolling over her cheeks instead of the excitement she had hoped to feel bursting from her chest.

She read about Mr. Johnson's visit and how rude Levi's father had been. She read about how Levi could no longer write and how he had no choice but to resign himself to a life on the farm with no stimulation with his love for words at all.

Her heart all but broke as he signed off at the end of the letter.

Through the hazy vision of her tears, she grabbed a pad of paper and pen and began to write. Levi couldn't give up and she wouldn't let him.

My dearest Levi

It breaks my heart to know that Mr. Johnson found your writing of such high regard. I do not know a lot about the business of books, but I do know that to be offered to be published after having only written a few chapters isn't something that happens often.

I saw something in your writing that called to me. Something that touched my heart in a way few books have done in the past. I did not mean to cause trouble for you when I sent the pages to Mr. Johnson. I was simply praying for a miracle.

And the miracle came. He liked it.

In my naivety I thought your daed would be proud, that he would finally understand that your love for reading wasn't just a hobby or a simple pastime to avoid farm work. I prayed he would understand that you have a true talent, one gifted to you by Gott himself.

I am sorry for the trouble I have caused. I apologize profusely.

But I am not allowing you to give up on your dream.

You are a writer, Levi, a dreamer. Gott gave you this talent to reach people you have never met. To use the written word to bring joy and wisdom to people of all ages and all cultures. Do not let your daed diminish what you feel or what you want to do.

Every night, I will pray that he will realize his mistake. I will pray that he understands how much the written word and writing means to you. I will pray that he realizes Abram is the rightful farmer. I will pray that he accepts you for who you are and not for who he expects you to be.

I pray for this Levi, because I know Gott has plans for you.

Open your bible and read Jeremiah 29:11. For I know the plans I have for you, declares the Lord. Plans to prosper you and not to harm you, plans to give you hope and a future...

The Lord will not make empty promises in his word, Levi. I know this with all my heart. You just have to keep faith and keep praying.

Just like I will.

I miss our visits beneath the tree, and Shakespeare misses his apples and fresh water. Although the widow Baker spoils him with sugar cubes, I see the way he longingly looks towards your farm when we pass by once a week.

Amos has begun building Mamm's dawdi haus, although it looks more like a cottage than a dawdi haus. She's elated to have a little place of her own. Amos also has a sweetheart, so I don't think it will be long before an engagement is announced in Sunday Service.

I so wish that I could tell you all of this in person, but I know it isn't possible. Instead, I will keep writing to you and sharing my thoughts on my latest reads.

Just this week I read a book about a man facing an unsurmountable challenge. He had lost his family, his work, and his friends all through a simple misunderstanding. The book follows his journey as he struggles to find the courage to continue to prove his innocence and how he wants to give up.

Just when he feels that all hope is lost, something happens that clear his name. Unexpectedly, without notice, he gains everything he had lost.

But during the hard times, he realized who were the real people in his life he could trust. It was a heartfelt book about the faces people wear when things are gut, and how their true colors shine when things get hard.

I know that even in the hardest of times, Levi, you are a rainbow to those around you.

Don't let your father dim the bright light Gott has given you.

Shine Levi, shine with all your might and keep writing.

Love,

Annie

P.S. Find paper and pencils included. Go on and write that next chapter.

Annie read the letter over once again and wondered if she should post it. If Levi's father were to find it, he was bound to be in even more trouble.

But she had to have faith that either Levi or hopefully his brother, Abram, would find it first. She kissed the envelope and said a prayer for it to find its way to Levi, before she tucked it into her purse to mail in the morning.

She might not be able to see Levi anymore, but that didn't mean out of sight, out of mind.

Instead, absence made her heart grow fonder.

Chapter 18
The Serpent &
The Light

It was mid-morning, and the sun was hotter than the days before. A brief shower of rain the week before had caused the weeds to bush around the base of the corn plants, and now Levi, Abram, and his father were trying their best to wage a war against weeds.

They worked on the edge of the farm, the last field before they gave way to the more rugged terrain of rocks and brush. As he tugged out the weeds, getting the roots as well, the sun shone down hard on his back. The scent of dirt and greens surrounded him, even as his father complained in the next row about how he had never worried about weeds before.

If it were up to his father, they wouldn't bother with the weeding at all.

But after Levi had taken the time to explain to Abram how much an overgrowth of weed could affect your crops—especially by luring in pests such as mice and rats, Abram insisted they all pitch in.

Just like every other day since his father had banned books on the farm, Levi worked in silence, keeping his head down and his mouth shut. He'd learned over the course of the last few weeks the quieter he was, the more pleased his father seemed to be.

Could Abram be right that his father felt threatened by his wisdom?

Levi wasn't sure, but for now his silence was keeping the peace.

He thought about Annie's letter he had received the day before and smiled when he remembered the pad of paper and pencils she had included. He had immediately hidden them under a loose floorboard to make sure his father couldn't confiscate those as well.

Just like the man in Annie's story, Levi was waging a war against insurmountable challenges, but unlike that man, Levi had yet to see the light.

He glanced up at the sun and squinted as the bright rays met his gaze. There was light. He just had to make his father understand that reading and writing weren't a sin. Perhaps if he asked the bishop to talk to his father... Levi mused as he tugged out another weed.

The next moment, he heard Abram cry out in pain.

Levi jumped up and rushed towards his brother, only to feel his heart stop when he saw what was happening.

A timber rattler had his brother by the lower leg, and instead of just letting it go, Abram was trying to stop the bite by grabbing the snake's head, inadvertently causing more venom to be injected into his bloodstream.

"Levi help!" Abram cried out desperately as he fought with the snake to let go of his leg.

Isaac rushed over to the commotion, but as soon as he saw what was happening, he froze right on the spot.

Levi took command of the situation instantly. "Daed, grab the spade. Abram let go of the snake. If you let go, it will release. Daed, as soon as the snake is free, I need you to kill it."

"No need, it's a corn snake, copperhead at most," Isaac argued faintly.

Abram let go of the snake, it's fangs released and it whipped its head back.

"Daed, now!" Levi cried out.

Isaac dropped the spade just behind the snake's head, looking mightily impressed with himself. "There it's done."

Before Levi could say another word, his father was at his brother's side. He had his pocket knife out and was ripping open the pants where the snake had gotten Abram. If Levi knew what his father was going to do next, he would've stopped him.

Before he could, Isaac sliced a three-inch cut into his brother's leg over the bite.

"Daed, what are you doing?" Levi cried out, horrified.

"My daed always said you need to bleed the venom out," Isaac said as if he were mightily proud of his memory.

Levi cringed, knowing that his father must have nicked an artery. Instead of slight bleeding, there was blood now spurting out of Abram's leg. "That's an old wives' tale, Daed. Abram needs to get to a doctor now! That wasn't a copperhead, it was a timber rattler. It's lethal if not treated and bleeding Abram out will not stop the venom from getting into his blood stream."

"Is there supposed to be so much blood...." Abram asked weakly as blood pooled around his leg.

Levi pulled off his belt and tied it around his brother's leg, just below the knee. He glanced at his father and said in a stern voice. "Grab the snake and run to the shanty, phone for an ambulance. They'll need the snake to know what anti-venom to give Abram."

"But I...." Isaac wanted to argue.

"Run Daed. If you don't want Abram to die, stop arguing and run."

Isaac thought for a split second before he grabbed the snake and ran.

Levi carefully helped his brother up and talked to him firmly. "Abram, I need you to stay awake and work with me. An ambulance can't get all the way out here in the fields. I'm going to carry you back, but you need to stay awake, you hear?"

"Everything's warm..." Abram said drowsily.

Levi knew his brother's blood pressure was falling, and the venom had begun its work. They needed an ambulance, and they needed one as soon as possible.

He slipped an arm around Abram's waist and all but carried him back to the yard, praying the entire way that his father had done as he had asked. For just once, he needed his father to trust his wisdom instead of feeling threatened by it.

Chapter 19
Blood is Thicker Than Water

Annie was driving through Old Apple on her way to Levi's community when the ambulance rushed past her.

For a moment she was afraid her mother's predictions would come true and Shakespeare would get frightened and overturn the buggy, but just as always, he was calm as a lamb. Instinctively, Annie said a prayer for whomever needed an ambulance before she continued on her way.

She wished she could stop by the Hertzler farm today. She missed Levi terribly, and after reading his last letter, she wanted to tell him in person how she beloved in him. But she knew that wasn't possible.

Levi's father was stubborn and judging by the way he had chased the Englischer away, he wouldn't think twice about chasing her away in the same manner.

So instead she thought of all the times they had spent together. The happy memories brought a smile to her face. She thought of the first time they had met, when she had steered Shakespeare into a ditch and how he had found her surrounded by books and in tears.

She thought back to their visits under the oak tree and how they discovered the joint love for reading and their admiration for similar authors. A smile curved her mouth by the time she turned onto the dirt road leading into his community.

The same ambulance that had rushed past her in town was now rushing back towards town. Sirens blaring, making it clear that it was a medical emergency.

It was only then that she looked ahead and saw the number of people gathered at the Hertzler farm. Annie's heart skipped a beat, fearing that someone had been hurt.

If it had been Levi...

Just last night, she had dreamed of sharing her future with him. Although they hadn't officially courted, she had fallen in love with him. Through their visits and their letters, she realized that Levi was the man she wanted to spend her life with.

She didn't want to be courted by someone at her Sunday singings; she didn't want a mann that her mother approved of; she wanted Levi.

She wasn't sure how he felt about her, but she knew in her heart that he also had affectionate feelings for her.

Annie snapped the reins and begged Shakespeare to go just a little faster, to meet the crowd standing at the Hertzler farm. She didn't recognize anyone, but stopped, regardless.

"What happened?" Annie asked, all but jumping out of the buggy as she approached the group of people.

A young boy, about age twelve, turned to her with a sad expression. "Timber Rattler, hadn't had one of those in these parts for years. Must've been the rain."

"A snake?" Annie cried out, horrified. "Where's Levi?"

"In the ambulance on his way to the hospital." The boy said before he turned and headed back to his parents.

Annie felt her heart sink into the dirt below her feet. Her breath came in shallow pants as she realized the enormity of the situation. A timber rattler bite could be fatal. If they didn't call the ambulance right away...

Tears burned her eyes, but she bit them back. She couldn't cry, not now. She had a long drive home, and she wasn't even sure what condition Levi was in. Perhaps it was all just a precaution. Perhaps the snake barely bit him at all.

But as she looked at the surrounding people, she could hear their murmurs and musings and it made her even more frightened.

"He was so pale."

"There was so much blood."

"So young, he hasn't even married yet."

"So much blood...."

"Do you think he's going to make it?"

"Was the ambulance on time?"

The questions made her tummy twist inside out. Bile rose in her throat, realizing that she might never see Levi again.

She realized it must have been a terrible bite for there to have been so much blood. She glanced at the cornfields beyond the barn and couldn't help but feel the anger rise inside her. If his father hadn't been so stubborn, if his father had only accepted Levi for who he really was, none of this would've happened.

She walked back to the buggy and took the reins. But instead of directing Shakespeare towards the house of the widow Baker, Annie directed him home.

Until she knew if Levi was all right, Annie wouldn't make for good company at all.

For one day, the traveling library wouldn't visit its usual customers, because today, its proprietor had a lot more on her mind than the books.

Her only thought was Levi and realizing how much she would regret it if she lost him before she even told him she had fallen in love with him.

It was a good thing Shakespeare knew the way home, because Annie all but cried the entire way.

When she finally arrived at home, her mother rushed out onto the porch, instantly knowing something was wrong.

"Annie, what's wrong—what happened? Are you hurt?" Rebecca asked hurriedly.

Annie shook her head. "It's Levi... a timber rattler got him. They say there was blood, Mamm, too much blood. They don't know if the ambulance got there on time."

She had yet to tell her mother about Levi, but right now just had to be the right time. She needed a shoulder, she needed sympathy, she needed her mother to understand how truly afraid she was.

"Levi, who is Levi, Annie?" her mother asked, confused.

"He's a mann, in the community south of town, Mamm. Daed use take him books, now I do... Mamm...." Annie sniffed and searched her mother's gaze. "I think I'm in love with him."

For a moment, Rebecca searched her daughter's gaze before she pulled her in and held her against her chest. "Ach, my poor dochder, I didn't know. I'm so so sorry. Kumm, I'll make you some tea, then we'll figure out how to find out if he's all right? Is that gut?"

Annie nodded gratefully. "Denke Mamm. He doesn't even know... he doesn't know how I feel."

Amos joined them and turned to Annie with a curious look. "That's the mann you told me has such a gift for writing."

Annie nodded. "That's him. The mann I hope to be courted by some day."

Her family huddled around her, supporting her, although neither of them had met Levi. In that moment, Annie knew that regardless of how angry, mad, unreasonable, or crazy your family was, they were still family when it mattered most.

Chapter 20
An Old Wives Tale

Levi and his father sat in the waiting area of the emergency room, while the doctors and nurses tended to Abram.

Levi had traveled with Abram in the ambulance, while his father had followed shortly after with one of their neighbors.

When the ambulance had arrived at the hospital, the doctors had rushed Abram into the back with the dead snake in a bag for identification. Levi had never prayed as much or as persistently in his entire life. He only hoped that he had done the right thing by creating a tourniquet around his brother's leg. If he hadn't, Abram might well lose his leg for good.

Fear gripped his heart like a tight vice, winding tighter and tighter with every passing moment.

His father sat beside him in complete silence, lost in his own fears and thoughts.

Now and then Levi glanced up at the clock on the wall expecting to see an hour had passed, just to be disappointed to learn it had only been another five minutes.

He had heard about timber rattlers, but he'd never seen one before today. He knew he would never forget the image burned into his memory when he'd seen Abram struggling to get the snake off, instead causing it to bite him repeatedly.

"Mr. Hertzler?" A man asked in a white gown, stepping into the waiting room.

Both Levi and his father jumped up. "That's me." They said in unison.

The doctor walked towards them with a neutral expression. Levi prayed his brother was still alive, and if so, that he still had his leg attached.

"Are you Levi?" the doctor asked Levi. "I'm Doctor Ahmed."

Levi nodded. "I'm Levi and this is my daed, Isaac Hertzler. He killed the snake."

The doctor nodded. "If it hadn't been for your quick-thinking Levi, your brother might not have made it to the hospital. You correctly identified the snake, and by binding a tourniquet around your brother's leg, you stopped a bleed, which would've likely been fatal."

"Is Abram all right, his leg…" Levi trailed off, eager to learn about his brother's condition.

"Yes. Abram is in recovery at the moment. We had to give him anti-venom, which is usually a feat just as dangerous as the snake bite itself. But he made it through with flying colors. We repaired the cut on his leg and repaired the artery that had been nicked. We'll need to keep him for a night or two for observation, but as of this moment, he is stable and won't suffer any long-term problems from either the bite or the wound."

Dr. Ahmed shook his head and sighed. "Whose idea was it to *bleed* the poison?"

"Mine," Isaac said immediately.

The doctor nodded with sympathy. "I realize that in many cultures, it's believed that bleeding the poison might save a life, but I'm afraid to inform you, it's never the right answer. A tourniquet, regardless of bleeding, stops the venom from traveling through the body. By letting someone bleed the poison, you could cause him to lose his life if you can't get a transfusion in time."

Levi felt sorry for his father as he went as pale as a sheet. Levi laid an arm over his father's shoulder. "Denke doctor. We'll remember that next time. Denke for all your help. Can we see Abram now?"

"In a while, a nurse will be in to collect you as soon as they have processed him for admission and moved into a room." The doctor smiled at them before he left.

Levi let out a grateful sigh of relief. "Denke Gott for a miracle."

His father didn't share the sentiments, instead he turned to Levi with a baffled look. "How did you know all that? How did you know to do the thing with your belt, or what type of snake it was?"

This was the last moment on earth Levi would want to fight with his father, but he wasn't about to lie. "I read about it in a book about reptiles and snakes found on farms."

"You read about what to do in case of a snake bite. I thought the books you read were all just made up Englischer nonsense," his father said, shaking his head, still looking confused.

"Daed, I do read fiction, but I also enjoy factual information. I enjoy learning about the world and how we have progressed to knowing more about our surroundings, animals, weather patterns, crop enhancements, and the odd medical journal," Levi explained hesitantly. He waited for his father's outburst, but it didn't come.

Instead, his father smiled sadly. "I'm glad you read a book about snakes before I prohibited them. You saved your bruder's life."

"You saved his life by calling the ambulance and killing the snake," Levi reminded him.

For the first time in what felt like years, Levi and his father shared a smile. A smile that spoke of truce, a smile that spoke of hope.

"Mr. Hertzler? You can come with me if you'd like to visit with Abram."

Together, Levi and his father followed the nurse. This time there were no unsaid words, no arguments, and most of all, no contention between them.

As soon as they stepped into Abram's room, Abram smiled weakly. "It's a gut thing I have a book worm for a bruder. The doc tells me if it hadn't been for you, I would've gone along with the snake."

Levi chuckled. "He's exaggerating."

This time, Levi felt his father put a hand on his shoulder. He didn't say a word, but the gesture was more than enough for him to experience the gratitude his father was trying to express.

Chapter 21
A Courtship or
a Breakup

Annie nervously tapped her foot against the floor. She glanced around the coffee shop and couldn't help but feel anxious about her reason for being there.

After the commotion at the Hertzler farm, she had told her mother everything about Levi. Instead of being angry about falling for a man from a different community, her mother seemed pleased that Annie had finally opened her heart to her future. Her mother sympathized with Levi's situation and even more because he and Annie weren't allowed to see each other again.

Her mother had helped her to contact the hospital to find out if Levi was all right. Annie was overwhelmed with relief to hear that the patient hadn't been Levi, but his brother Abram instead. Immediately she had penned Levi a letter, sending well wishes to his brother and asking to be kept abreast of his recovery from the snakebite and the nasty cut on his leg.

She hadn't heard a word from Levi in a week. He hadn't answered her letter, or even attempted to contact her.

Instead, Annie had resorted to calling the hospital every day until they released Abram.

She couldn't help but fear that Levi's father had finally tightened the noose and was forcing Levi step up and take over the farm.

That was until she received a cryptic letter from him yesterday. He didn't speak of books, or about missing her, or even about Abram's recovery. Instead, the letter just asked her to meet him at a coffee shop in Old Apple at noon today.

It was only eleven forty-five, but Annie was too wound up to wait at home another minute before driving Shakespeare and the buggy into town.

"Would you like something to drink?" a waitress interrupted her thoughts.

Annie nodded. "Just… kaffe please." Annie shook her head. The last thing she needed now was more caffeine. "Nee, please, just a glass of juice would be fine."

The waitress moved and revealed Levi standing behind her.

Annie's heart skipped a beat as she took him in. It had been almost a month since she'd seen him in person. She couldn't remember him being this attractive, or his eyes sparkling with such joy at seeing her. It made her chest swell with hope, but, this could also be their last goodbye.

Last night she had dreamed he was only asking to meet her to tell her he won't be writing to her anymore.

"Hullo Annie." Levi's voice was deep and warm and although Annie feared why he asked her to meet him here, she couldn't help but feel happy to hear him say her name.

"Hullo Levi," Annie said carefully as he took a seat. "How's Abram?"

"Back on both feet and now more than ever before convinced that weeding is the answer to keeping pests, including snakes, out of his cornfields," Levi said with a wry smile.

Annie frowned. "His cornfields?"

"That's why I wanted to see you, Annie. The news I have is simply too gut to not tell you in person," Levi said, reaching for her hand.

Annie's mind spun a million miles a second as his warm hand folded over her smaller hand. "News?"

"You told me to pray for a miracle in your letters, Annie. I did. I prayed every day, but after a while I thought that Gott wasn't listening anymore. And then when Abram was bitten by the snake... I never thought a miracle could come in the way of a timber rattler biting my bruder."

"How was that a miracle? That was a disaster!" Annie cried out, confused.

"Because my knowledge of the snake and how to treat Abram saved his life. My daed finally understands that my love for knowledge, reading, and writing isn't a threat to him or his position in the family. He finally understands it's simply who I am."

"You mean... I can stop by with the traveling library again?" Annie asked hopefully.

Levi nodded with a broad smile. "I'd like that very much. But I have more news. Yesterday, I went to see Mr. Johnson."

"The publisher?" Annie asked, crossing her fingers beneath the table.

"Jah. Annie I signed a book deal. I received an advance and I have a contract for four more books. I no longer have to rely on the farm for an income. My father officially gave the farm to Abram last night. I'm free to pursue my future and Abram is free to take over the farm just like he's always wanted."

Annie was speechless. Tears of joy welled in her eyes. "Levi, that's the best news ever. I'm so, so, so happy for you."

"That's not all," Levi said, leaning closer. "My daed also gave his blessing so I could court a girl from another congregation. He's asked permission from the bishop and it has been granted. So I was hoping, on Saturday, we leave the book buggy and Shakespeare behind and instead I take you on a buggy ride in my buggy?"

Annie's smile spread from ear to ear. "Levi, you want to court me?"

"I've been hesitant to make my feelings for you clear, given the situation I was in. But now, I'm free to tell you, Annie, that I fell for you that very first day you were sitting in the dirt crying with books in your lap."

Annie chuckled through the tears of joy. "I fell for you the moment you gave Shakespeare an apple. My mamm always said a mann that is kind to animals has a gut heart."

"I'd like to meet your mamm," Levi grinned.

"You will, this Saturday, when you pick me up for our buggy ride," Annie promised as the waitress returned with two glasses of juice.

Levi lifted his glass in a toast and smiled at Annie with love in his eyes. "To miracles, to books, and to a future so bright, only Gott could've planned it."

Epilogue

"It's a letter from Mr. Johnson," Annie said as she set the letter down in front of her husband.

Levi smiled at her as he opened the letter and read.

"Kumm, read faster. Tell me what it says?" Annie asked anxiously as she poured them each a cup of coffee.

After being married to Levi for the last thirteen months, Annie still found her husband just as handsome, intriguing, and brilliant as the very first day they met. Their lives differed greatly from the other Amish people in their community, and yet they were as much part of the community as anyone else.

They had a kitchen garden, a small barn with a cow to keep Shakespeare company, and a small coop of chickens for fresh eggs. But they didn't have farmlands, or plows, or spend their days working in the fields like most of the members of their farming community.

Instead, they spent three days a week on the traveling library Annie had inherited and the other three days they remained home. On the days they were home, Levi would write, while Annie would catch up with housekeeping chores.

The cottage they lived in had come available for sale shortly after their engagement. At first, they had been hesitant to invest Annie's inheritance in a property, simply because Levi felt it was his responsibility to provide them a home. But Annie insisted the property was perfect. Besides, with Levi's advance, they could live comfortably until the release of his next book.

The cottage was only two miles from Annie's family, which meant they could still visit her mother often, and it wasn't too far for Levi to help at the Hertzler farm, when Abram needed a little manpower.

And it was theirs.

That was the best part.

Over the last year, they had created their own routines and had fallen in love with each other a little more each day. If Annie had ever thought that the love stories she had read from the traveling library were exaggerations, she now realized they were anything but.

In fact, she wished she had Levi's talent to put their story into words. And he did. It had been a bestseller, just like Mr. Johnson had predicted.

"And..." she nudged him as she set down his cup of coffee down on the table.

"He says it's another winner. He's just waiting for the final chapters before he sends it for editing," Levi finally answered with a smile. "I was so afraid Annie..."

Annie understood her husband better than anyone else. After he had achieved such outstanding success with his first novel, he feared that no other novel he wrote would ever live up to it. His latest novel had been a Christian-inspired story about a lost child finding a family. It had been a story written from his imagination, with a flair of faith that only Levi could infuse into fiction.

He had been waiting for weeks to hear from Mr. Johnson, and now that he had, Annie knew it was the right time to share her own news with him.

"That's wunderbaar Levi, your daed will be so proud," Annie gushed.

It was still hard to believe that the man that had all but tried to drown Levi's love for the written word had now become his fiercest supporter. Every chapter Levi wrote, he first took to his father to read. His father had become a critic, a voice of reason, and a cheerleader in every way. It warmed Annie's heart to know that the father-son bond that had been so close to being damaged forever had been repaired.

She also knew that it had been another miracle that Gott had blessed them with.

"I know. I'm just grateful the bishop made an exception for the typewriter. Without it, I don't think I could've kept up writing by hand." Levi smiled as he reached for his coffee.

Annie laughed. "Then you would've rested your hands and I would've written while you dictated."

"You're a gut frau Annie," Levi said, reaching for her hand.

Annie smiled at him, feeling her heart burst with joy and excitement. "And you're a gut mann, but you'll make a wunderbaar daed."

Levi smiled before his smile turned into a frown. "A daed?"

"In about seven months, jah," Annie said, watching him digest the news.

"We're having a boppli?" Levi's face exploded with joy.

"We're having a boppli," Annie agreed, "and judging by Mr. Johnson's letter, another best seller as well."

"To think none of this would've happened if you hadn't continued with the traveling library?" Levi said, shaking his head in awe of the decision that had led them to this moment.

"Hah!" Annie laughed. "I still wonder if you would have fallen in love with me if I hadn't nearly turned over the buggy."

Levi chuckled with a twinkle in his eye. "Perhaps not, but there were still the book recommendations. No one understood my mind like you, no one still does. We were fated to find each other, my frau." Levi's voice was filled with love.

Annie nodded. "Fated through faith and led by prayer."

*** The End ***

Thank you kindly for choosing to read my book. I sincerely hope you enjoyed it. All of my Amish Romances are wholesome stories suitable for all to enjoy.

If you could be so kind to leave a review on Amazon, I would appreciate it.